THE HOUSE ON SUNRISE LAGOON

BOOK TWO

Marina in the Middle

ALSO BY NICOLE MELLEBY

Camp QUILTBAG (with A. J. Sass)
The Science of Being Angry
How to Become a Planet
In the Role of Brie Hutchens . . .
Hurricane Season

THE HOUSE ON SUNRISE LAGOON

BOOK TWO

Marina in the Middle

NICOLE MELLEBY

ALGONQUIN YOUNG READERS   2023

Published by Algonquin Young Readers
an imprint of Workman Publishing Co., Inc.
a subsidiary of Hachette Book Group, Inc.
1290 Avenue of the Americas
New York, New York 10104

Printed in the United States of America
Design by Neil Swaab

The publisher is not responsible for websites (or their content) that are not
owned by the publisher.

LIBRARY OF CONGRESS CATALOGING-IN-PUBLICATION DATA
Names: Melleby, Nicole, author.
Title: Marina in the middle / Nicole Melleby.
Description: First edition. | New York : Algonquin Young Readers, 2023. |
Series: The house on Sunrise Lagoon ; book 2 | Audience: Ages 8–12. |
Audience: Grades 4–6. | Summary: On a quest to become someone's favorite
Ali-O'Connor, ten-year-old middle child Marina enlists Boom, her new neighbor,
to help make a documentary about her, but when things do not go according to
plan, Marina begins to wonder if she will ever feel like she belongs.
Identifiers: LCCN 2022050444 | ISBN 9781643753119 (hardcover) |
ISBN 9781523523801 (paperback) | ISBN 9781523523818 (ebook)
Subjects: CYAC: Middle-born children—Fiction. |
Anxiety—Fiction. | Belonging—Fiction. | Family life—Fiction. |
Lesbian mothers—Fiction. | Documentary films—Fiction.
Classification: LCC PZ7.1.M46934 Mar 2023 | DDC [Fic]—dc23
LC record available at https://lccn.loc.gov/2022050444

ISBN 978-1-64375-311-9 (hardcover)
ISBN 978-1-5235-2380-1 (paperback)

10 9 8 7 6 5 4 3 2 1
First Edition

THE SUNRISE LAGOON SERIES
IS DEDICATED TO KRESTYNA LYPEN,
EDITOR EXTRAORDINAIRE,
WHO HELPED ME BRING THIS FAMILY TO LIFE.

THE HOUSE ON SUNRISE LAGOON

BOOK TWO

Marina in the Middle

THE SECOND RULE OF BOATING:
ALWAYS BE MINDFUL OF OTHER BOATERS.

CHAPTER ONE

Marina Ali-O'Connor watched her sister Samantha stand at the edge of the dock in their backyard. Sam had a small Ugly Stik in her hand, one of Mom's old fishing rods, which she kept reeled up. Small fish had been jumping in the lagoon all morning, leaving ripples behind on the surface of the water. This had the Ali-O'Connors' Great Dane, Good Boy, barking his head off, so he had since been banished inside.

So far, Sam had caught nothing. She cast her line for the hundredth time and slowly reeled it back in. All five of the Ali-O'Connor siblings, as soon as their hands were big enough to hold a fishing pole, had been taught how to bait, how to cast, and how to reel to catch many different kinds of fish.

"Sam, you're too close to the edge," Marina said from her perch farther back. Marina, at ten years old, was a year younger than her sister, but she seemed to have much better self-preservation skills. Plus, she wasn't yet used to seeing Sam standing on the deck without a life jacket on. Sam had just recently learned to swim. She'd been the only one of the Ali-O'Connor siblings who hadn't known how. Marina couldn't even remember learning. She'd just always been able to.

Their moms made sure the kids learned as soon as possible. Water safety was important, and Mom was chock-full of rules to make sure no one would ever get hurt. Especially since the Ali-O'Connors lived in a house right on the water in New Jersey. Instead of a backyard with grass, they had a deck, a dock, and the lagoon. Mom's three boats were tied up to the dock. The *Sunrise Princess*, which Mom used to charter fishing expeditions, was the largest. *Harbor Me* was the boat they used most often as a family to take rides across the bay. And *Raggedy Ann* was the smallest, the oldest, the most rusted and busted. According to Marina, *Raggedy Ann* was nothing more than a death trap. Mom didn't seem to agree.

Though in Marina's opinion, all the boats were giant floating death traps.

"Sam! You're too close. Step back!"

The shout caused Sam to cast an awful line, and she groaned, reeling it back in. "Stop, Marina! I'm fine."

Marina didn't understand why Sam, who had until recently been so afraid of swimming, didn't seem to be afraid of *anything* now that she'd learned how. It was like a switch had been flipped the moment Sam successfully made it across the bay unassisted, and every single thing she was scared of had disappeared.

Marina wished she could access her switch. Lately it had been flipped in the exact opposite direction. "Sam!"

"You aren't my *mom*, Marina!"

"Oh, hey now." Mama's voice rang out along the back deck. Voices carried easily across Sunrise Lagoon. It was why they always knew exactly what their across-the-way neighbor Brenda Badger was thinking. It was why they knew that Jamie Perez, the teenager who lived a few houses down, got in trouble for missing her curfew all the time. And, until about a week ago, it was why they couldn't do anything without sending the Patels' dog into a frenzy. The Patels had lived in the house on the corner, but they'd recently moved.

The Ali-O'Connors would miss the Patels, but nobody on Sunrise Lagoon would miss their dog.

"As one of your *actual* moms, who wants to tell me what the trouble is out here?" Mama asked. Even though breakfast had been over for a while, Mama was still dressed in a pair of Mom's plaid pajama pants. They were too big on her narrow waist, sitting low on her hips. She always stole Mom's clothes. She claimed they were more comfortable.

"Marina is smothering me," Sam said.

"Sam's too close to the edge, and not even wearing a life vest, and she's only been swimming for, like, not even a month, and—"

"Sweet girl, it's not your job to police your siblings," Mama said. Marina had been known to carry on forever if they let her. "You let *us* worry about Sam."

"But—"

"No buts," Mama said. "Though also, Sam, I would appreciate a heads-up if you're going to be out here. You're still a new swimmer, and I'd like to keep an eye on you. Yes?"

Marina resisted the urge to stick out her tongue and say *I told you so.*

"Yeah, okay," Sam mumbled. She turned her back on them to cast again.

Mama stayed outside to watch for a bit. Sam, with her white-blond hair and freckled pale skin, was the odd one out of the three of them. Besides Sam, the only other blonds in the family were Harbor, the oldest Ali-O'Connor sibling by four months, and Mom, their other mom. Not that Marina looked very much like Mama when you looked close enough. Sure, they both had dark hair. Mama's, though, was a rich black, and it was curly, just like the twins'. Marina's was every shade of brown, thick and wavy. She barely knew how to handle it, even though it was hers. Currently, it was piled up high on her head in a ginormous bun. The twins, like Mama, were part-Syrian. Sam was Dutch, just like her biological grandmother, who was currently living in an assisted living home. Harbor was half-German, from Mom, and half-Italian, from her dad.

Marina was, according to her adoption records, Mexican, from her birth mom, and something else, from her birth dad. She didn't know what that "something else" was, since her birth dad's name wasn't in the records, and all her papers said was that she was "mixed race." That was what happened sometimes when you were adopted as a baby, like she was.

The back door slammed open against the wall of the house. The twins, seven-year-old Lir and Cordelia, the youngest Ali-O'Connors, came barreling out. They ran barefoot across the deck, Good Boy following at their heels and barking loudly.

"Mama! There's a moving truck!" yelled Cordelia. She had the loudest voice of them all, so now the entirety of Sunrise Lagoon had been alerted to the truck's appearance.

"Don't run on the deck," Marina shouted back. Her heart was beating faster and faster as she watched the twins. Cordelia, especially, was prone to spills, and the deck was made of wood panels that were easy to trip on. *No running on the deck* was one of Mom's rules, and the twins knew better. "Mama, tell them!"

"We're not running. We're just standing here," Cordelia said, after they had come to a stop on the other side of Mama.

Mama shot them a look. One that said, *Your sister is right, but I'm not taking her side right now.* At least that was Marina's interpretation. Most of the time she was certain that Mama loved the twins best.

"Relax, sweet girl," Mama said. She wrapped an arm around Marina's shoulders, but Marina shoved it off.

"We should go to the park instead of worrying about the new neighbors," Marina said. She was always trying to convince her family to go to the park a couple blocks away. It was located by the boat ramp where everyone launched their boats into the lagoon, but it was far enough away from the water to feel safe.

"Do you think the new neighbors will have kids?" Cordelia asked, pointing across the lagoon to where the Patels had lived. There was indeed a large white moving truck parked there.

"Maybe," Mama said.

Marina was doubtful. The Ali-O'Connor siblings made up almost the entirety of the child population on Sunrise Lagoon, other than Jamie Perez, who was seventeen and pretended the Ali-O'Connors didn't exist, and the three Badger brothers—George, Sonny, and Pork—who stayed with their grandparents for the summer. The Badgers would be here for only two more weeks before they would go back to Staten Island to start school again. Harbor, who was best friends with Sonny Badger, was growing increasingly grumpier as that date grew closer.

And Harbor was already the grumpiest of the siblings.

Something clattered to the ground behind them, and Marina jumped. Her heart sped up. It had been doing that a lot lately.

"Oh no!" cried Cordelia.

A piece of Frankencrab had fallen onto the deck. Frankencrab was her most prized piece of art. It was a giant sculpture of a crab made from *actual bits of crabs*. Mom had been eagerly awaiting the day when it finally crumbled. Unfortunately for her, besides this piece, it was staying strong.

Marina closed her eyes and took a deep breath, trying to get her heart back to normal. When it got like this, beating fast, fast, fast, it reminded her of seagulls' wings when they tried to fly against the strong bay wind. When she opened her eyes again, Mama was looking at her with a soft, curious expression. Marina ignored it.

"I should go fix it," Cordelia said.

"There's Krazy Glue in the shoebox under my bed," Lir said.

"Excuse me?" Mama said. "How about you give me that Krazy Glue when you're done, Cordelia."

Cordelia took off running back toward the house. Marina tried very, very hard to ignore her this time.

A loud *bang* came from across the lagoon as the movers began unloading the truck. Good Boy, picking up the slack for the Patels' now-absent dog, began barking his head off. Mama and Marina watched in silence as Sam reeled in her fishing line to come stand with the others.

They all wanted a glimpse of the new neighbors. Most of Sunrise Lagoon had been there for years and years. Mom had grown up in this house, and moved back into it with Mama when Harbor was a baby. Almost everyone else had been there, it seemed, just as long. The Patels were moving to Florida, where they were retiring. That was what usually happened if someone moved out. The majority of Sunrise Lagoon was older people—like the Badgers, across the way, and Mr. Harris and Mr. Martin, who both lived up the street.

Everyone on Sunrise Lagoon knew everyone else's business. They would know these new neighbors' business, too, soon enough.

The door opened, and Mom came outside. Mama cringed as the door hit the house again. Good Boy went over to whine at Mom's feet. She was usually the one who walked him. He probably didn't need to go out now. He just liked the treats Mom gave him afterward. She petted his head, ignored his pleas, and went to stand with the rest of her family.

Mom wrapped an arm around Mama's waist and pressed a kiss to her cheek. She wrapped her other arm around Sam. In Marina's opinion, if Mama's favorites were the twins, Mom's were definitely Sam and Harbor.

"I'm gonna head out to Joe's to do some repairs this afternoon," Mom said. "What're we all looking at?"

"The new neighbors are moving in," Lir explained.

The door slammed open again.

"Can you all please open that door more carefully?" reprimanded Mama as Sonny Badger and Harbor came running outside.

"And can we all *stop running*, please?" mumbled Marina.

"We just saw the new neighbors," Harbor announced. The entire Ali-O'Connor clan turned away from the lagoon to look at her and Sonny. "They're surprisingly not old! Or, well, still old, but not *that* old. Maybe Mom's age."

"Gee, thanks," Mom said.

"But that's not all," Harbor said, smirking. She loved knowing something no one else in the family did. "They've got a kid! And not an annoying teenager like George or Jamie, and not a little kid like the twins and Pork—no offense, Lir."

"Some taken."

"Our age?" Sam asked.

"I think maybe more like Marina's," Sonny answered.

That made Marina's heartbeat speed up again. Just like the seagulls' wings. *Flap, flap, flap, flap*—right against her chest.

"Well," Mom said, giving Marina a wink. "I think that sounds wonderful."

As they watched the movers take furniture and other boxes out of the truck—things belonging to someone who might actually be her age—Marina absolutely, one hundred percent, did not agree.

CHAPTER TWO

During the school year, bedtime in the Ali-O'Connor household worked like a well-oiled machine. Mom made sure everyone brushed their teeth and were in bed when they were supposed to be: eight thirty for the twins, and nine for Marina, Harbor, and Sam. Mama made sure everyone had clothes picked out for the next day so there weren't extra distractions in the morning that might make them late for school. Mama was also the one to read the twins a bedtime story.

Marina, Sam, and Harbor could read for a bit in bed if they wanted, but no screens. Marina would have liked to join the twins for story time, but she never said anything. She felt like a baby as it was, sharing a room with both of her older sisters.

But once summer began, every single organized moment of bedtime went out the window. With all the holidays, parties, and boating events, bedtime became more of a suggestion than a rule. When the day was done and the sky was dark and the kids were tired, that was when they'd go to sleep. Or, sometimes, when Mom decided they were cranky or underfoot and needed to go to bed.

Tonight was one such night. Harbor and Cordelia were the cranky ones. Harbor, with all the outrage of an eleven-year-old, had been arguing with their moms about needing her own bedroom.

"Would you like me to build you a new bedroom?" Mom had said. "Perhaps we can knock down the wall in the kitchen and put it there." Mom usually dealt with Harbor's more difficult moments through sarcasm.

Mama didn't always approve. She usually tried to find actual solutions. "We have what we have, Harbor. If it's privacy you're craving, let's talk about that. We can find ways for you to get some alone time."

Neither answer was good enough for Harbor, who was huffing and puffing in her bed. She was loud enough that it was downright annoying.

"Harbor, stop it," Marina said.

"Leave me alone," Harbor replied, her usual refrain.

Earlier, Cordelia—after a long day swimming in the lagoon with Lir and their neighbor Pork Badger—kept spontaneously bursting into tears over every little thing. Now, she was throwing a seven-year-old tantrum in the twins' bedroom. Both moms were trying to calm her down. This happened every so often. Cordelia, who loved to play outside, refused to acknowledge when she was tired and should stop.

It was creeping up on eleven o'clock, which was an unheard-of bedtime, even in the summer.

Marina, Harbor, and Sam were still waiting for one of their moms to pop in and say good night. Harbor kept huffing and puffing, and Sam, who must have been getting a summer cold, was breathing loudly through her mouth. Both of which annoyed Marina, who couldn't wait to turn on her sound machine. It played white noise, like a spinning fan, and blocked out everything, all the other noise and the worry, so that maybe she could sleep.

The house was small, and their bedroom was smaller. Marina could hear every creak, every breath, every summer breeze against the window. Sam tossed and turned a lot, and Harbor sometimes snored. Plus, Harbor had hung a large poster of WNBA star Diana Taurasi over her bed, and the first thing Marina saw when she woke up were Diana's intense eyes looking right at her.

Honestly, Marina sometimes wanted Harbor to have her own room, too. Mostly so that Harbor and her poster of Diana Taurasi wouldn't keep Marina awake at night.

There was a soft knock on the bedroom door. The Ali-O'Connor house was a "knock before entering" house, and mostly everyone followed that rule. (Except for Cordelia, who often conveniently forgot.)

Mom popped her head in. "You three settled in here?"

She was answered by three very unenthusiastic groans of confirmation.

"Try and get some good sleep tonight. And maybe consider having an easy day tomorrow, all right?" Mom said. "You've been nonstop this whole summer. Take a break."

"But we've only got like two more weeks before school starts and the Badger brothers go home," Sam pointed out.

"I don't want to talk about that!" wailed Harbor.

"Hey, okay. Good thoughts instead," Mom was quick to interject. Harbor would be unbearably moody for days after Sonny went home. It was best to keep her spirits up, however possible. "Why don't we go tomorrow and pick out lights for the boat, for the Labor Day parade. That sound good?"

Labor Day weekend always brought mixed feelings. It was the very last few days before school started. It was also a big holiday for the Ali-O'Connors. They'd have a barbecue that could rival the Fourth of July. It was the last party of the summer, so everyone would be there, and it was the final time for months that their moms wouldn't worry about what time they went to bed. Most importantly, they would take part in the Parade of Lights. It was magical: when the sky turned dark, everyone on Sunrise Lagoon dressed up their boats in colorful lights, like a house on Christmas, and drove them down the lagoon and into the bay.

Marina remembered Sam watching all the sparkly, bright

boats with tears in her eyes the very first summer Sam had been with them. "What's wrong, sweet Sam?" Mama had asked.

Sam had whispered, "They're just so pretty."

Marina did not share that sentiment.

"Yeah, I guess," Harbor said now, in response to Mom's question about helping her pick out lights for this year's parade. Harbor sounded surly, but the eagerness in her eyes gave away her enthusiasm.

"Me too," Sam said. Because of course she wanted to go. Boats were her thing. Boats were Harbor's thing, too. Both of them wanted to be Mom when they grew up.

Marina sighed. Stringing up the biggest boats on the lagoon with a ridiculous number of lights just seemed dangerous. She may have been ten, but she was smart enough to know that electricity and water didn't make a very good mix.

Marina pictured the whole family, including Good Boy, surrounded by twinkling lights with staticky sticking-up hair and smoke coming out of their ears.

So when Mom asked, "How about you, Marina? We could use all the help we can get if we're going to beat Mr. Martin this year," Marina said, "No, thank you. I think I'll take a day to rest instead. Like you said, we've been going nonstop all summer, and I really am tired, and my sound machine has been making a weird crackling noise lately, so maybe I need a new one, so I haven't been sleeping that great, either, and—"

"Okay, okay," Mom said. "But I hope you know I expect you to be on the *Princess* for the parade. Family tradition."

"I didn't have to come on the Fourth of July, though. Maybe you can just drop me off at the park, where I can watch you—"

"There won't be anyone staying behind to watch *you*," Mom said. "And, honestly, Marina, this is getting ridiculous. We're going to have to start talking about why you won't go on the boats anymore."

"I just don't want to," Marina said.

A simple explanation. She just did not want to.

That was all that mattered. Not the way her stomach hurt when she thought about going on the boats. Not the way she found it super hard to breathe when Mom stayed out longer than she said she would. Not the way she kept learning more and more ways that just being in the bay, at the beach, on a boat, could hurt you.

No. All that mattered was that she did not want to, and that was all her moms needed to know.

"We'll talk about it with Mama later," Mom said, and then she turned out their bedroom light. "Get some sleep, my little fishes. I'll see you in the morning."

"Good night," Sam said.

"'Night," Harbor said.

Marina didn't bother also wishing Mom good night. She figured, with everyone else saying it, the point had been made.

She did, however, glance up at the Diana Taurasi poster and whisper "Good night" to it before rolling over and reaching to turn on her sound machine. But just as she was about to press the button, Harbor said, "They're gonna make you see a therapist or something if you keep being weird."

Marina scowled at her. "I'm not being weird."

"There's nothing wrong with seeing a therapist," Sam said.

"That's not what I meant," Harbor said. "My point is, we live on the water. You've been around the boats your entire life. It's *weird*, Marina."

Marina turned to Sam to appeal for help. Earlier that summer, Sam and the oldest Badger brother, George, had gotten each other in a lot of trouble when they'd stolen George's grandparents' small motorboat. "I don't understand how you can crash a boat and nearly drown and be fine with getting back on one."

Sam sat up in the bed, her forehead creased. "So you *are* scared, then?"

"There's nothing to be afraid of," Harbor said. She was using her *I'm the big sister, so you should listen to me* voice. "Nothing bad has ever happened on our boats. Mom knows what she's doing. Nothing bad ever happens during the Parade of Lights. Nothing's going to go wrong."

Marina gasped. Harbor had absolutely jinxed them. "Well, now, something definitely is going to go wrong, because you said it wouldn't!"

Harbor groaned. "Oh my god, never mind. Just go to sleep." Then she rolled over. Conversation done.

That suited Marina just fine. She didn't want to talk about this anyway. She reached again for her sound machine.

Apparently, though, Sam wasn't done yet. "Marina?" she said.

"What?"

"I just think that, since we live on the bay, and the boats are such a big part of everything . . . well, maybe you should consider trying to figure out how to get back on them again," Sam said. "The boats are who the Ali-O'Connors are. Don't you want to be a part of that, too?"

Marina didn't respond. She turned her sound machine on so no one could talk to her, and she wouldn't hear them even if they tried.

CHAPTER THREE

The next day, Marina was on a mission. Harbor and Sam were out with Mom, and Mama had taken Cordelia and Lir grocery shopping. (It would be a miracle if Mama didn't return with way more snack food than she wanted, in part because Cordelia had a tendency to *wander*.) Marina had a limited window while the twins were gone.

Frankencrab needed to go.

Their moms were being way too nice about the giant crab made out of shelled crabs. Cordelia may have worked exceptionally hard on her deranged artwork, and Lir may have gone through the painstaking job of cleaning out all the shells, but enough was enough. It was falling part, and Lir's job wasn't perfect. Some of those shells were starting to smell. Seagulls had been swooping down closer and closer lately to get a good look. The chances of getting pooped on had gone up exponentially since Frankencrab had been banished outside.

Marina stood on the deck with a large black garbage bag in her hands. She shook the bag out. Good Boy, who had followed her outside, tried to nip at the bag as it blew in the wind. "Good Boy, stop. I have to move quickly before Cordelia and Lir get home!"

They would be upset, sure. The rest of the family, however, would absolutely thank her later.

Marina wasn't thrilled about touching Frankencrab, but luckily Lir kept a stash of gloves in the twins' bedroom. She'd helped herself to a pair. She'd also taken Sam's cell phone to listen to the playlist she'd made the last time she had "borrowed" it. The worst part about having older siblings was that, to keep things fair, when they got something for their birthday—like cell phones on their eleventh birthday—the rest of them had to wait until their *same* birthday, too. Marina, unfortunately, had only just turned ten.

She turned the music up as loud as it would go and kicked her flip-flops off so she could dance along the deck without tripping over her shoes. She wasn't a *dancer* or anything, but she enjoyed the distraction of the music, and she liked to bop along with it.

Now, as she swayed side to side with the rhythm, she needed to decide how to best pull Frankencrab apart. She didn't want it to come crashing down on top of her. Good Boy, who had been sniffing Frankencrab—and Marina's feet—ran to the edge of the dock and started barking. Marina turned around and spotted Pork Badger across the lagoon with a fishing net in his hands. He was scooping it into the water, trying to catch jellyfish. At least the littlest Badger boy, unlike his older brothers, wouldn't make fun of her dancing.

"Hey! Across the way! Hello! You have nice moves! What are you listening to? What are you doing?" someone shouted. "My name is Bernadette, but you can call me Boom!"

The voice from what used to be the Patels' back deck was so loud the entire neighborhood had probably heard it. It startled Pork, who nearly lost his footing, which startled Marina, who was ready to start screaming if he fell in.

He didn't fall in, though. Marina exhaled and turned to face the source of the shouting.

It was a girl. She stood on the deck in a bright-yellow tankini, hands cupped around her mouth so she'd be louder. Eventually, she would learn that she didn't need to work so hard to be heard across the lagoon.

"I'm Marina," Marina said when Boom continued staring at her, apparently waiting for a response.

"My name is Pork," said Pork.

"Why do they call you Pork?" yelled Boom.

"I don't know," Pork replied. "Why do they call you Boom?"

"My grandma says it's because I'm a firecracker!" she shouted.

Good Boy was barking his head off at all the screaming.

"You don't need to yell," Marina said, using her best indoor voice to prove it. "We'll be able to hear you just fine."

"Oh. Interesting," Boom said.

She was white, *really* white, too pale for summer on the water—she looked like she'd get a sunburn at any second—and her hair was light, like hay, and short, falling above her shoulders in straight strands that blew in the wind but then fell immediately back into place. Marina, with her hair all piled up on top of her head, was jealous.

"Well, hello, then," Boom said. "I won't yell anymore! How old are you?" She was still yelling a little.

"I'm ten," replied Marina.

"Me too! Awesome! Hey, I like your dog. I have a cat. His name is Amato. What's your dog's name?"

"Good Boy."

"That's not a name. Those are adjectives."

"I think 'boy' is a noun."

Boom paused, thinking. "Well, if you use it to describe someone, like 'Look at that boy Pork Chop over there,' isn't it an adjective?"

Marina's head was starting to hurt a bit.

Pork, at that moment, caught a jellyfish. He pulled it up, and all three of them watched as its spineless body squished and dripped right through the net, coming out the other side completely whole again and falling into the water.

"Whoa," Boom said. "That was awesome! Do that again. Let me record it!" She had a cell phone in her hand, and she put it in camera mode, turning it to face Pork. "Okay, I'm ready."

"They aren't easy to catch," Pork said. "Give me a sec."

With the two of them preoccupied with catching jellyfish, Marina decided she'd better get back to her task. She figured she would start with the pieces that had already fallen off Frankencrab, and began picking them up from the ground.

"What are you doing?" called Boom.

Marina sighed. "Throwing away this monstrous thing."

"Cordelia is going to be mad if you do that!" said Pork, leaning from the deck to peer into the water. Marina wanted to yell at him to be careful.

"Which one is she?" Boom asked. "While we were moving in, I watched about a million people go in and out of your door. How many families live in that house with you anyway?"

Marina's stomach squeezed.

"Just the one," Pork said, his voice fraught with confusion. "Just the Ali-O'Connors."

"Oh," Boom said, sounding equally baffled.

It seemed Marina was the only one who wasn't confused at all. That didn't mean she wanted to explain it, though. In fact, she didn't want to be out here at all anymore. "I have to go," she said, and without waiting for Boom to respond, she added, "Bye."

She turned on her heel and went inside.

Frankencrab was safe for now.

CHAPTER FOUR

The Ali-O'Connors were what you would call a "conspicuous family."

All the children knew what that meant, and Marina had heard lots of stories. It meant that Mama could be taking Sam for a visit to her grandmother, and a random person in the lobby of the assisted living home might say, "Your husband must be exceptionally blond for your daughter to be so light-haired!" Or Harbor could be in the middle of a basketball game, with both her moms in the crowd cheering for her, and a newer teammate might ask, "Which one of them is your real mom? I mean, which one of them gave birth to you?"

It meant that if they were all together at the diner, with two moms and everyone looking very different from one another, someone a table over might say, "Your family is wonderful. Did you adopt all of them?"

There were different ways of making a family, but one look at the Ali-O'Connors, and everyone automatically knew they weren't the easy-to-explain, biological kind.

Their moms had told the kids that, most of the time, people didn't ask questions or make comments to be rude but that the kids didn't always have to respond to them. Cordelia and Lir always did, though. They loved to teach strangers how the Ali-O'Connors had become a family. Harbor *hated* to respond, since she had a dad who was still in her life, a situation she thought needed more explaining than everyone else's.

Marina disagreed. At least Harbor knew exactly where she'd come from. At least Harbor didn't have to deal with people saying, "Do you speak Spanish?" since Marina was Mexican. And Harbor didn't have to see their confused faces when Marina replied, "No."

Luckily, though, Marina had been going to the same school since kindergarten, and everyone in her class understood that Marina was adopted and Marina had two moms. She'd also always lived on Sunrise Lagoon, where she knew her neighbors.

Or, at least, they used to. Marina hoped someone else would explain everything to Boom. Maybe she would ask one of her siblings to.

They were all sitting around the table for dinner. Marina, as always, was squashed between Harbor and Mom. While the twins, who sat across from them, had plenty of room, the same could not be said about the side Marina was forced to sit on. The table was really big enough for only six of them. To fix that problem, Mom sat in a folding chair.

Lir was currently picking at the dinner. Mama had made shakshuka, and Lir was pushing the tomato chunks to the edge of the dish.

"Eat those, Lir," Mama said. "They're just tomatoes. You like tomatoes."

"I don't like tomatoes in my sauce."

"Sauce *is* tomatoes," Harbor said.

"I don't like the chunky ones! I don't want the chunks." Lir scooped up the runny parts of the sauce, ate the feta and the eggs, and continued making piles of the tomato chunks.

Marina pushed the food around her plate, as well. "I met the girl across the lagoon," she said. Everyone turned to look at her. Marina didn't often speak up during dinner. There was too much chaos to bother. "She asked how many families live here."

"I told you we need a bigger house," Harbor took the opportunity to say. "One with more bedrooms so I can have my own room."

Mom laughed. "Oh, come on. There's not that many of us in here."

Mama gave Marina a sympathetic look. Marina blushed. As much as she wanted to be understood, she didn't want Mama to be the only one who did understand. "That's not what she meant," said Mama. "Was it, Marina?"

Marina shrugged.

"What did she mean?" Cordelia asked.

"Oh, I get it. She probably thought me and Mom and Sam were one family, and Cordelia and Lir and Mama were another, or something, right?" Harbor said. "Well, just tell her to mind her own business. That's what I do."

"Or you can just explain it to her," Mama said. "Some families are different, and that's perfectly okay. You all know this, right?"

They all nodded their heads. Good Boy, from his spot by Mom's feet, whined for food.

"What about me?" Marina asked.

"What *about* you?" said Mom.

"Harbor said you and her and Sam would be one family, and Mama and Lir and Cordelia another," Marina said. "So which family am I?"

"This one." It was Sam who answered. "It's just one family. It's just us."

That wasn't what Marina meant. What she meant was that Mom and Sam and Harbor were white and loved boats. Mama and Lir and Cordelia were part Syrian and shared DNA. And then there was Marina. Still, she didn't feel like arguing. They all went back to eating their dinner, and Mom apologized to Good Boy, since there wasn't anything in shakshuka that she could share with him.

The rest of dinner went smoothly enough. Lir didn't eat the

tomato chunks, so Mom finished them. Good Boy eventually realized he wouldn't get anything from Mom's plate, so he went to eat out of his bowl in the corner of the kitchen. Everyone cleared their own place at the table, and it was Cordelia's turn to help wash the dishes. Usually, that meant Mama would wash and Cordelia would dry, and then Mama would dry them again so that they really *were* dry before putting them away.

But when Cordelia went to take her spot by the sink, Mama said, "Go ahead, Cordelia. Mom and I need to speak with Marina, so you're off the hook for tonight."

Cordelia heaved a great big relieved sigh. Then she scrunched up her nose at Marina and said, "Sorry," and booked it out of the kitchen before either mom could change their mind.

Marina sank low in her seat. "Why do you want to talk to me? Because of Boom, across the lagoon? It's fine. I just didn't want to explain everything to her—that's all."

"It's not that," Mom said. She patted Marina's leg from her spot in the folding chair. "We wanted to talk to you about the boats."

"I don't want to talk about the boats."

"Marina, sweetheart, this has been an issue for you all summer," Mama said. "We just want to try and understand."

Marina narrowed her eyes. "Maybe I don't *want* you to understand," she snapped.

Hurt flashed across Mama's face. Marina saw it but chose to ignore it. She'd been snapping at Mama a lot lately. It seemed like everything Mama said made Marina mad. She didn't know why. She didn't know why she didn't snap the same way at Mom, either.

"Maybe it's just because I don't want to go on the boats. I don't have to like going on the boats just because you all do, you know. I'm allowed to have other interests, even if Sam and Harbor only want to live and breathe the boats. Because—"

"I'm going to stop you there," Mom said. "There's a difference between you not caring about boating and you refusing to go on the boats at all. The Parade of Lights is in less than two weeks. It's the very last time we'll be on the boats as a family this summer, and I want you there. I really do. And if you really won't, we think you should talk to someone. Like a counselor, like Sam does."

"But there's nothing wrong with me!"

"And there's nothing wrong with Sam for seeing her counselor, either," Mama was quick to say. "We aren't trying to punish you. We just want to understand what you're afraid of."

Marina's stomach was squeezing really tightly right now. Her heart was beating fast, fast, fast, a wiggling fish pulled onto land. She quickly stood up, her chair skidding backward on the floor. Good Boy barked at the sudden movement. "Why can't you just leave me alone?" Marina said directly at Mama, taking a page out of Harbor's book.

"Hey, now, watch your tone, little fish," Mom said.

Marina's heart fluttered faster and faster. It made her start breathing kind of funny, too. "I don't want to talk about this anymore," she said. "*Please*," she added for good measure.

Luckily, her moms took pity. "Okay," Mama said. "We won't talk about this anymore tonight. But we are going to have to keep talking about this."

Marina ignored her, glancing at Mom instead. "Please?"

Mom sighed. "Go ahead. Go wash up."

Marina didn't wait to be told twice. She left the room as fast as she could, running away from the conversation.

Marina had managed to go the entire summer so far without having that conversation. When she'd made up reasons for why she didn't want to go fishing with Mom, or for a cruise down the Forked River, or across the bay to Tices Shoal, her moms had tried to get her to change her mind, of course. They'd tried asking her what was really going on. But Marina had been very careful to keep her tone light—very no-big-deal—hoping they would drop it altogether. It was almost Labor Day. It was almost the end of the summer. Marina just had one more boat trip left to avoid.

Then she'd be able to breathe again, without having to worry about the boats until Memorial Day.

She needed to find a way to get herself back off her moms' radars. She needed to lie low. She made a point of making her bed in the morning. She didn't argue with Sam for finishing the milk before Marina could have some in her cereal. The Ali-O'Connor was a big, loud family. Marina just needed to blend into the background, like normal, until the summer came to an end.

Which was why, the next day, she decided to walk Good Boy alone when he started crying at the door, and she was the only one besides Mom and Lir sitting in the living room. "I'll go with you," Mom said.

"I can do it," Marina said, because if Mom went with her, then Mom might want to chat, and Marina did not want that. She moved quickly, grabbing poop bags (three of them, just in case, because Good Boy was a big dog) and the leash, and ushering Good Boy out the door. If Mom wanted to go with her, she'd have to catch up, so she probably wouldn't bother.

Of course, once Marina was outside, she nearly turned Good Boy back around. Not that she'd have been able to. Once Good Boy decided he was doing something, it was impossible to get him to do otherwise.

There, in the middle of the street, was Boom. And Good Boy was headed straight for her.

"Oh no," Marina said as Good Boy tugged her arm with the leash, effectively walking Marina instead of the other way around.

"Oh, thank the stars. It's you!" said Boom. She had her phone out, camera facing the ground in front of her. There was something there—maybe a crab. Marina couldn't tell from where she was. "Does your dog eat turtles? Keep him away if so! But can you go stand up there in the center of the street and make sure to stop any cars that come this way?"

Standing in the middle of the street to block cars sounded like a terribly dangerous plan. "No, thank you."

"I don't want this turtle getting run over," Boom said. "It's a box turtle, I think. Do you know? What kinds of turtles do you get over here?"

"Just move it. Quickly."

"I want to film it first."

Good Boy whined, pulling Marina toward the edge of the marsh next to the road so that he could do his business. "I think you should stop taking a video," Marina said. "You *and* the turtle are going to get squashed if you keep doing that."

"I like to document cool things that happen," Boom said.

Marina wasn't sure a turtle crossing the road should be considered a "cool thing." "Here, hold Good Boy's leash," she said. "I'll move it."

"Can I record you while you do?" Boom asked.

"Only if you also keep an eye on the road and yell if a car is coming."

"You've got it, boss."

Marina didn't trust that Boom would keep her safe from oncoming traffic, so she had to move quickly. With careful fingers, she reached down to pick up the turtle. It was brown, and it tucked its head into its shell as her shadow fell over it. She picked it up carefully, holding it by the edges of the shell and running as fast as she could to the side of the road. She flung it into the marshes. It hit with a splash.

"Whoa," Boom said. "I wasn't expecting you to send it flying. I'm glad I got that on camera. I want to zoom in later to the turtle's face."

Marina took the leash back from Boom. Good Boy immediately tugged her along the road, wanting to continue his walk. Boom followed right behind them. She still had her phone camera out.

"Why are you filming?" Marina asked.

"Just in case something awesome happens. Or a story comes up. I'm a documentary filmmaker, you know."

"Well, I'm definitely not a story, so you might want to save your battery."

"I actually came out here to film the funny-looking birds," Boom said, pointing at the blue heron that was perched in the marshes in the distance.

The blue heron's neck was stuck out long, like a little bird version of a giraffe. Lir compared them often to pterodactyls when they flew over the lagoon because of their exceptionally large wingspan.

"Thanks for the assist with the turtle," Boom said. "True documentarians aren't supposed to interfere with their subjects, but, well, I couldn't stand the thought of it becoming roadkill."

Good Boy stopped to do his business, so Marina and Boom stopped, too.

"I wish I moved here earlier in the summer," Boom said, "but my mom says I should be glad to be able to get settled before school. Where do you go to school? Maybe we'll be in the same class. Do you like documentaries? What do you want to be when you grow up?"

Marina didn't actually know the answer to that last question. Not like the rest of her siblings. Lir wanted to be a marine biologist, and Cordelia wanted to be a different kind of scientist (a mad scientist, if you asked her). Sam and Harbor both wanted to take over Mom's charter work someday, and repair boats, just like she did. "I'm not sure what I want to be," Marina answered.

"You could dance professionally."

"Oh, no. What you saw yesterday was all I can do," Marina said. "I just like it."

Boom nodded, as if that made perfect sense. "Well, not everything you like needs to be a career. My mom says having hobbies is good, and that I should have more. Oh! Do you want to come over after you walk your dog?"

Marina did not. "Oh, well, after I walk him I need to feed him. Plus, I haven't showered yet, so I probably should do that. And then my mom might need help making dinner. And then, well, maybe it'll be too close to dinnertime, so I'll need to eat dinner. Then maybe it'll be too late, because, well, it's after dinner, so . . ." Marina let the end of the sentence hang. Usually by now, her family would have cut her off.

Boom did not cut her off. She nodded as Marina rattled off her reasons. "Okay. How about tomorrow?"

"Tomorrow?" Marina said. "Maybe."

"Okay, great. I'll come see you tomorrow, maybe," Boom said.

When Marina got back to the house with Good Boy, Mom was waiting there with a treat. She had been watching Marina from the window the entire time. It made Marina feel like a baby. "Down, Good Boy," Mom said.

Good Boy sat down. Mom rewarded him with the treat. She petted him on the head, and then wrapped an arm around Marina. "Looks like someone made a friend out there, huh?"

Oh, Marina thought.

Was that what had just happened?

CHAPTER FIVE

Even though Marina had made zero commitment, and even though she was quite certain "Maybe" didn't mean "Show up at my doorstep bright and early the next morning," that was exactly what Boom did. She rang the bell in the middle of breakfast. Cordelia answered the door. "Hi, I'm Boom!" said Boom. She was loud enough that everyone at the kitchen table eating the scrambled eggs Mama had made could hear her.

"Hi, I'm Cordelia!" said Cordelia, just as loudly. "We're about to put our bathing suits on and go swimming. Do you want to come?"

That was how Boom joined the Sunrise Lagoon kids, swimming with the Ali-O'Connors, and Sonny and Pork, in the lagoon.

Mama sat outside with a bottle of water, watching them. Sonny lounged on a floaty that looked like a unicorn, and

Harbor lounged on one that looked like a swan. Sonny had a tight grip on the swan's wing so that he and Harbor would stay together as they bobbed up and down in the waves the others were making. Sam practiced somersaults under the water. She wasn't very good at them, since she couldn't get her head under her body to make a complete circle, so instead she spun around like a wriggling eel. Cordelia, Lir, and Pork were jumping and splashing around on a giant inflatable mat, which worked almost like a water trampoline as it bobbed with the motion of the bay.

Mr. Martin and Mr. Harris, who were best friends and lived next door to each other a few houses down from the Ali-O'Connors, were loading Mr. Harris's boat with fishing poles and nets. They waved at the kids, who waved back.

"Good luck out there," Mama called over.

"If we have a good day, we'll bring you over some dinner," Mr. Martin called back.

Boom was splashing on the mat with the younger kids. Then she belly-flopped into the bay. She swam over to Marina, who was lying on a towel on dry land, like usual.

"Are you coming in?" Boom asked.

"Nah," Marina said. She had her sunglasses on, her head tipped up to the sky. It was one of those quintessential summer days: sunny and blue, with big white puffy clouds casting shadows every so often. She had tried to talk her siblings into going to the park instead of going swimming, but it hadn't worked. So here she lay. "I'm very happy just lying here. It feels good, and I really enjoy sunbathing."

"Cool," Boom said, and then sprawled out on the ground right next to Marina, arms touching. They lay like that, in what Marina considered comfortable silence, for about five minutes before Boom said, "Want to come over to my house?"

No, she did not want to do that. But Marina made the mistake of glancing over at Mama, who was sitting on a lounge chair, legs tucked underneath herself, watching them. Marina thought she would be better off watching her children in the water. But Mama must have thought Marina was asking for permission, even though she was not, because she said, "I think that sounds like a great idea."

And Marina couldn't very well get out of it now.

"Fine. Okay," Marina said.

The first thing Marina noticed when they walked into Boom's house was that it was *quiet*. It was never quiet at the Ali-O'Connors', unless you were one of the first to wake up in the morning, which Marina never was. "Are your parents home? Because if they aren't, I really shouldn't be here. So we should maybe go back and—"

"Mom!" called Boom. Her voice echoed in the small, nearly empty house. Marina decided the house was quiet only when Boom wasn't home. "I made a new friend! Come meet Mariana!"

"*Marina*," Marina corrected.

"I mean Marina!" yelled Boom.

"Oh, that's a pretty name for someone who lives by the water." Boom's mother appeared in the hallway. She was a very tall woman. Harbor, who was pretty tall but still dying for a growth spurt to help her basketball game, would be jealous. She was also exceptionally put-together. She wore a flowy sundress that clung to her hips and waist, and her hair was pulled back in a bun that was decidedly not giant. Not like Marina's monstrosity on the top of her head. Every hair out of place on Boom's mom's head seemed like it had been purposefully placed there.

Marina considered explaining that she, Harbor, and Cordelia and Lir (who were named after the gods of the sea) got their names from things related to the ocean. But Sam, of course, was not, since she had been adopted at eight years old. So Marina would have had to explain their family as a whole. Which was far too much to tell a stranger.

Instead, Marina simply said, "Thank you."

"We're going to go to my room," Boom said. She grabbed Marina's hand and tugged her up the stairs. Her mom didn't ask a million questions, just waved them off as they disappeared to the second floor.

Boom's room was almost empty. There were boxes in the corner exploding with clothes, and her bed had a soft purple comforter on top of it, but otherwise, the walls and carpet were bare. "It's boring, I know. I'm still unpacking and stuff."

"I like it," Marina said, looking around it. "It's so clean and fresh and new, and you can do whatever you want with it. All four walls are for you."

"What does your room look like?" Boom asked.

Messy and crowded.

"I share it with Sam and Harbor. Sam has all her pictures, of her and her grandma and of her and our family, on the dresser. Harbor has a giant poster on the wall. I like my bed just fine, but the room mostly looks like it belongs to my sisters."

Marina sat down on the bed. A loud *mrowl!* rang out from underneath her, and a small black-and-white cat came barreling out from under the comforter. "Yikes!" exclaimed Marina, jumping back up.

"That's just Amato. You can pet him if you want. He's friendly!"

Amato perched on top of Boom's desk, glaring at Marina. She didn't think he'd appreciate her touching him right now. "Maybe later," she said. "Your mom seems nice."

"She's okay. My dad's more fun. He likes to make movies with me, but he works all the time. He'll be home later," Boom said. "Maybe you can meet him then."

"My mom works a lot lately, too. She used to work at home, but she just started working at another marina. She fixes boats there," Marina said, and then rolled her eyes. "My other mom has the summer off, though, because she's a teacher, so she's *always* around lately."

Boom tilted her head. "Oh," she said. "You have two moms?"

"Well, I guess I have three, technically. Kind of. I have a birth mom somewhere. I was adopted," Marina explained.

"Your moms are gay, though?"

Marina's stomach squeezed. "Yeah."

"And you're all adopted?"

Marina sighed. Part of her wanted to take Harbor's advice and tell Boom to just mind her own business. She didn't, though. "No. Just me and Sam. Harbor is my mom's biological daughter. She used to be married to Harbor's dad. And then my mama gave birth to Cordelia and Lir."

"How?" Boom asked.

"With a sperm donor," Marina said, and then she blushed, as she did every time she had to talk about this.

"Huh." Boom flopped onto her bed. Marina perched beside her. "Are the big boats tied up to your dock your mom's then? The one who fixes boats?" Boom sat up and pointed out her window, where she had a full view of the Ali-O'Connors' backyard. They could hear the squeals and splashes coming from the rest of the family, who were still in the water.

"The big one is called the *Sunrise Princess*. The medium one is *Harbor Me*. The rusty old one is *Raggedy Ann*."

"I've never been on a boat before," Boom said. "Would your mom take us on one? Can we go on one? Please?"

Just when Marina thought she was done talking about things she didn't want to talk to about, of course Boom would be interested in Mom's death machines. "Um. Yeah. She takes people out on the boats all the time. I'm sure you could go with them."

Boom frowned. "But not you?"

Marina sighed, a full-body sigh. "I don't like going on the boats anymore."

"Oh. Why not?"

Amato had crept back across the room. He sat right on top of Marina's feet, looking up at her expectantly. She reached down to scratch his ears. It was what Good Boy liked best. Amato started purring. "Did you know there are over seven hundred deaths a year because of boats? And over three *thousand* injuries. And, seriously, have you ever seen *Jaws*?"

"Not yet. My dad said we could watch it together, though," Boom said.

"*Don't.*"

"Well, but . . . it's just a movie. I can show you the behind-the-scenes stuff of the mechanical shark, if you want."

"But didn't you hear me? Boating accidents happen all the time, and I just don't like those odds," Marina said.

Boom was fiddling with her phone. She pulled up the camera and held it to Marina's face. Marina tried to duck out of the way. "So, what you're saying is, you're afraid."

"I guess. Yes. Why are you filming me?"

"Because it's a good human story, like my dad would say. Facing your fears! Don't you think your moms would make

-41-

sure you didn't get hurt? I mean, you have two of them. And, like, a billion siblings. That *helps* your odds," Boom said.

Marina found herself admitting something she had never, ever admitted out loud to *anyone*, before. "I'm the *last* one anyone would think about saving. You'll see. Sam and Harbor are Mom's favorites, because they love the boats. Plus, Harbor was here first. And Mama has the twins. She wanted to have them more than anything, you know. Even though they'd already adopted me."

"You're smack-dab in the middle," Boom said.

Marina sighed again. "I wasn't supposed to be. But then came Sam."

Boom was still recording her. Marina held her hand up to cover the camera lens. It did not deter Boom. "I think we should make a documentary. I think we should get you to overcome your fears and get you back on a boat by the end of the summer. I'll direct."

Marina shook her head. "That sounds like an awful idea."

Though maybe it wasn't. The Parade of Lights was at the end of the summer, the last big boat-related family event. Her moms would be proud and happy if she joined them, and then she wouldn't need to see a counselor. And she wouldn't be the odd one out anymore. Like Sam said, boats were a big part of who the Ali-O'Connors were, and Marina *did* want to be a part of that, too.

Still, she approached the situation with the appropriate level of skepticism. "Well . . . okay, maybe. How?"

Boom stopped recording. She got very still and very quiet, which looked unusual on her. Her forehead creased, and she bit her lip. "You know what? I don't know. But that's okay! Lots of documentary filmmakers don't know how the story will unfold until it does! In the meantime, we can brainstorm. And we'll meet again soon." Boom nodded definitively, but then her entire face changed. Her voice was much softer as she asked, "Right? We can meet up again, right?"

For once, Marina couldn't come up with a single excuse. "Yeah, okay. Let's brainstorm and meet up again."

CHAPTER SIX

The next morning, Marina lay on her bed, staring at Diana Taurasi on Harbor's wall and contemplating life. She daydreamed that Mom's boats disappeared into thin air. She daydreamed that Mom came home and suddenly declared, "You know what? You're right. The boats are dangerous, and it was irresponsible of me to suggest you go for rides on them! Let's all go to the park instead!"

She daydreamed that Boom made a world-famous documentary about her. It won an Oscar and everything. Her family was impressed.

The house wasn't as quiet as Boom's, but it was as quiet as it ever got. Mama was taking Harbor for her annual sports physical, and the twins were supposedly across the street at the Badgers'. She didn't know where Mom and Sam were, but it probably had something to do with the boats, because that was all they cared about. Which left Marina alone in the bedroom with neither of her sisters, a very rare event and why she was inside and not outside, enjoying another picture-perfect summer day.

"I'm going to hang my own poster one of these days," Marina told Diana Taurasi. "And if you come to life in the middle of the night, like I suspect you do, whoever is on my poster will defend me. I'm considering Godzilla."

The poster of Diana Taurasi did not respond.

The sound of bare feet padding quickly down the hallway echoed through the bedroom. They went from louder to softer, as whoever it was ran in the opposite direction. Then the sound got louder again, as if they'd come running back. This repeated three times before there was a knock on Marina's door.

"What?" Marina said.

The door swung open. Lir stood on the other side, glancing anxiously around Marina's room and clinging to the doorknob, twisting it back and forth. "I can't find Mama. Or Mom. Do you know where they are? Do you know where anyone is?"

Marina shrugged. "Probably outside with the boats, with Sam. I thought you were hanging with Pork."

"I was, but I came home to get out of my bathing suit, because we were inside, and it was still damp, and I didn't like how it felt. But. I messed up." Lir's face was scrunched up, his eyes watery.

Marina didn't want to deal with tears, but she asked, "What happened?"

Lir was breathing loudly. "I took my suit off, and I put it on my bed, by accident. And I didn't know, but it had something on it. Something green? I don't know! But it's all over my comforter, and I need someone to wash it. Now. Fast."

Marina climbed out of bed. "They're probably right outside. Hang on. Come with me."

Lir followed Marina as they crossed the house and looked out at the back deck. No Sam nor Mom. Marina turned around and realized Good Boy was nowhere to be found. His leash wasn't where it was usually hung up, either. "They must be walking Good Boy. They'll be right back, then."

This didn't comfort Lir. "I need to wash my blanket. I need Mama to wash it. It's wet and green. I don't like it, Marina."

"Well, okay. Let me take a look."

Lir followed Marina down the hallway to the twins' bedroom. They stood in front of Lir's comforter, which was stained with wet, green muck. Lir's bathing suit was on the floor, and when Marina kicked it, she confirmed that whatever had gotten all over Lir's bed was indeed all over the swimsuit, too.

Lir was starting to cry.

"Help me take your comforter off," Marina said. Lir, who didn't like touching dirty things, ran to get gloves, and the two of them bunched the comforter in their arms. "Grab the bathing suit, too."

They carried the bundle into the laundry room, which was really just a section of their garage. Marina opened the washing machine and shoved the comforter inside. Then she threw Lir's bathing suit right on top. She climbed onto the washing machine so she could reach the cabinet above it, where Mama kept the detergent. Luckily, she found some pods, so Marina didn't have to guess how much to put in. She figured one was enough, and threw it in with the comforter and bathing suit.

"Do you know how to start it?" Lir asked.

Marina did not, because she and Harbor, and even Sam, had been ignoring Mama every time she told them they needed to learn how to help with the laundry. But how hard could it be?

There were a bunch of knobs. She just had to figure out what setting she should choose. The first knob was for water temperature. Marina wasn't sure what to pick, but she thought it might be like taking a shower. She turned it to HOT.

"What if that's too hot?" Lir said.

Marina turned it to WARM to be safe.

The other knob gave her four options: REGULAR, HEAVY, DELICATE, and LIGHT. She figured REGULAR was her best bet. The last thing to do was to hit START and hope for the best, so that was exactly what Marina did.

They waited until the lid of the washing machine locked, which she figured meant there was no turning back. Then Marina heard the water rush in, and everything *seemed* to be going normally. "That should do it," Marina said.

Lir was wiping away tears. "Oh, good. It was making my stomach hurt. And it was making it hurt here, too, by where I breathe."

Marina watched Lir carefully. "I know what you mean. I sometimes feel that, too. Like it was too hard to breathe the right way? Like everything was getting too tight?"

Lir nodded enthusiastically. "Yes! Just like that! And it still hurts a little bit now, but not as bad now that you're washing my blanket. Thank you, Marina!"

Lir hugged Marina tightly around her middle, face squashed against her. For all either of them knew, the blanket could come out worse than when it had started. She hoped that wasn't the case. She hoped she was able to help Lir, because she knew the feeling that Lir felt. It was the same way she felt thinking about the boats. She hadn't known that anyone else ever felt that way, too.

The front door opened, and they could hear Good Boy scramble into the house, begging for his treat. Mom's and Sam's voices drifted inside, and Good Boy's leash clanked as they took it off him. Lir darted out of the laundry room. "Mom! Mom, Marina helped me wash my comforter, because it got really messy. But it's okay. We cleaned it!"

Mom came rushing into the laundry room, needing to see for herself that chaos hadn't occurred, that the room wasn't covered in bubbles or water. She leaned over and inspected the settings. She looked impressed as she placed a hand on

Marina's shoulder. "Nicely done. Maybe next time just wait for me and Mama, though, okay?"

"Can I go back to Pork's?" Lir asked.

"Yeah, go ahead. Just be back for dinner," Mom said, and Lir ran out of there before she had even finished talking.

The front door opened again, and Mama's and Harbor's voices joined in with everyone else's. The quiet of earlier that morning was gone, and now both Sam *and* Harbor were home to take over the bedroom if they wanted.

Marina glanced back at the washing machine as it rumbled and spun and cleaned Lir's comforter. *At least*, she thought, *there's one person in this family who sometimes feels just like I do.*

Even if there was a big difference between worries about a messy comforter and boating disasters.

CHAPTER SEVEN

Mama made lemonade. In Marina's opinion, she didn't add enough sugar. She told Mama this as everyone else guzzled down their drinks.

"You could add more sugar to your own, if you must," Mama said.

"Or you could actually make it right to begin with," Marina replied.

Sam made a choking sound.

"I think it's good, Mama," Cordelia said. She proved her point by finishing her entire glass in one giant gulp. "Ah!" she said, exhaling dramatically, the top of her lip shining with lemonade.

"Of course you do, because Mama makes everything exactly how *you* like it," Marina said.

"Marina, I think you need to go outside, and away from the kitchen," Mama said. All the kids knew that really meant, *I need you to go outside, and away from me.*

Luckily, the doorbell rang at that exact moment, and Boom appeared, saving Marina from further argument. Mama poured Boom a glass of lemonade, and she followed Marina out the front door to sit on the porch swing.

They sipped their drinks and swung gently, watching the boats in the distance drive across the bay. The marshland was peppered with white egrets.

Boom, of course, was the one to break the silence. "I wish I'd arrived sooner. I clearly missed something. The atmosphere was *tense*."

Marina shrugged. "It wasn't anything."

Boom took a big sip of lemonade. "This is really good, by the way."

Marina scowled.

"Anyway . . ." Boom put her cup on the porch and pulled out her phone. She held it up to Marina's face. "I'm actually here on business."

"Why are you filming me?"

"Reaction shots," Boom said. "I was thinking about what you said about boat accidents and *Jaws* and stuff. Actually, it gave me nightmares, so thanks for that. But! What if I could guarantee that someone would make sure you were safe if anything happened? Wouldn't that make you feel a little better about going on the boats?"

"Um . . . Well, I guess. But how?" Marina reached out to push Boom's phone down.

"We just make sure you're someone's favorite. Then you'd be the first one they'd protect. Like, if Amato and a regular cat were both on the roof of the house for some reason, I'd be waiting on the ground as Amato's safety net. I mean, I'd be worried about the other cat, too, but Amato is my favorite *everything*."

"But I already told you—I'm not anyone's favorite *anything*."

"Maybe not now. But we can *make* you someone's favorite. One of your moms, or one of your siblings. We just need to figure out what to do so they like you best, and then they would *absolutely* be your safety net," Boom said. "And then you wouldn't have to worry, because that someone would have your back."

Marina paused to think. Could she become someone's favorite? Could she be Mom's? Or Harbor's? Or Sam's? "It might take a lot of work," Marina said. "What if we don't have enough time to make sure I have a safety net before the parade?"

"Hi, Marina."

Marina and Boom looked up to see Sonny Badger standing in front of them.

"Is Harbor home? Or Sam? I was waiting out back, but they didn't come outside," Sonny said. "Maybe they're busy?"

Marina pointed at the front door. "They were in the kitchen, last I saw. You can go look for yourself."

Sonny nodded, hesitating for a moment before opening the door and disappearing inside.

"He's a strange boy," Boom said.

"He just has a crush on my sister."

"Which one?"

Marina shrugged. "I don't know, but it's definitely one of them."

"Well, anyway, back to the plan. We don't know if it will work unless we try. And I'll record us every step of the way. It'll make a documentary, and the footage can also help us learn what's working," Boom explained. She started fiddling again with her phone. "I'm gonna make a list of director's notes on here. Who do you think would be most likely to be your safety net? We can start there."

"I don't know," Marina said.

"Do you want to start with one of your moms?"

Mama seemed unlikely. And Harbor and Sam had been competing over Mom since Sam had joined the family. They fought about who would take over Mom's business so much it had caused problems earlier this summer. Throwing Marina's hat into that competition seemed exhausting.

"Maybe I should start with one of my siblings," she said.

"Okay. What does your oldest sister like best in the whole wide world?"

"Besides herself?" Marina said, and then immediately thought about Diana Taurasi on their bedroom wall. "Probably basketball."

"Hey, Miss Marina!" It was Mr. Martin calling her from his front porch. He had on a floppy fisherman's hat and an old shirt with a fishing pole on it that said KEEPIN' IT REEL. Mr. Martin was an older white man, gray and wrinkled. His wrinkles, though, lining his eyes and mouth, were mostly because all he ever did was smile. He was considered one of the grandpas of Sunrise Lagoon. "We're about to start a game of cards," he said. "We could use a fourth player. You in?"

"Only if me and Boom can be a team!"

"The more the merrier," said Mr. Martin.

That was how Marina and Boom ended up sitting at the card table in Mr. Martin's sunroom, with Mr. Martin, Mr. Harris, and Ms. Leisha Stewart, who lived a few lagoons up but sometimes joined in for card games. Mr. Harris was white, tall, and bald. He didn't have as many laugh lines as Mr. Martin, but he was working on getting them. He had moved in a little over a year ago, and he and Mr. Martin had become fast best friends. One was rarely seen without the other. Mr. Harris was the lagoon's newest grandpa.

Mr. Martin's sunroom was full of fish, hanging all along the walls. Not live ones, thank goodness, but dried-out ones. He also had a bunch of tuna tails over the doorway. Boom was really interested in those, and she pulled out her camera to take video. They could hear the rest of the kids splashing in the bay, and music coming from Jamie Perez's Bluetooth speaker.

Mr. Martin dealt the cards. "Does your friend know poker?"

Boom shook her head.

"Don't worry," Marina said. "I've been learning all summer. I'm getting really good."

"Keep an eye out on Harris, here," Leisha Stewart said. She was an older Black woman, with a smile full of teeth. Marina liked when she came to play. She always conspired with Marina against the men. She winked at the girls. "He cheats."

"I do not!" said Mr. Harris.

Marina leaned to whisper to Boom, "He really does."

"Just deal the cards," Mr. Harris grumbled.

Marina had spent a lot of time this summer with Mr. Martin and Mr. Harris. Usually when her family went out on the boats. Cards were fun, and safe, and Marina liked to impress Mr. Harris and Mr. Martin. Sometimes they even played with pennies, and so far this summer, Marina had won seven dollars and thirty-seven cents.

Mr. Martin turned on the music, and Mr. Harris got the game started. Boom immediately took out her phone to record, and didn't seem particularly interested when Marina tried to explain the rules. They studied their cards and placed their bets, tossing pennies into the center of the table, all while laughing and dancing in their chairs. Marina couldn't hear music and *not* move, and her chair kept skidding, bumping into Boom. Unlike Harbor, who would have pitched a fit, Boom didn't seem to mind.

Leisha was the big winner of the day, and once her lead was big enough, she said, "I should get home and figure out what to make for dinner."

"You just don't want to give us a chance to win our money back," Mr. Harris said.

"I'd be worried she'd beat you by even more," Boom said. "That was wild!" she told Leisha. "You were so good!"

Leisha laughed. "I like this one."

"We just moved in."

"Good. More girls to outnumber these two." Leisha winked at Boom and Marina.

They all helped clean up, but before Marina and Boom could leave, Mr. Harris stopped them. "Marina, remind your mom we've got that fishing trip this weekend. Our luck's been awful, but I know she'll help us turn that around."

"No one's better than that mama of yours," Mr. Martin said.

"Mom," Marina corrected.

"What?"

"Mama is the other one," she said. "But I'll remind her for you."

The sun had gotten even stronger when Marina and Boom stepped back outside. They shielded their eyes and began the short walk to their homes.

"That was so much fun," Boom said. "I didn't even know my neighbors at my old house. I'm so glad we moved here."

Marina smiled. "Me too."

When Marina got home, Harbor was watching a WNBA game. They were so rarely televised that Harbor was allowed to be in charge of the TV when they were. Harbor had ranted multiple times about the TV's lack of coverage of women's sports. It was best to let her watch whenever she could.

Harbor was on the living room floor, too close to the TV for Mama's comfort. She'd asked Harbor to sit farther away twice already, but Harbor hadn't moved. Good Boy enjoyed the company on the floor, showing Harbor his belly so she would scratch it. Mom was sprawled out on one of the sofas, her eyes shut and her feet kicked up as she snuggled into the cushions.

Marina listened to the sounds of the water running in the kitchen sink while Mama did the dishes, the squeak of the sneakers of the basketball court, and the loud noises of the crowd. If she was going to try to become Harbor's favorite, this was a perfect opportunity. Without saying anything, she took a seat on the other couch, curled her feet underneath her, and started watching the game.

She had no idea what was happening. The players kept moving back and forth across the court. Baskets were made, points were tallied, but it was mostly just a lot of running, if you asked Marina's opinion. She didn't even know who was playing. Maybe she should ask. "Is, um, Diana Taurasi playing? The one on your wall."

"No," Harbor said. She didn't offer any other information.

"Um. Who are we watching, then?"

"The New York Liberty and the Chicago Sky," Harbor answered.

"Oh," Marina responded. "Who do we want to win?"

Mom chuckled. Her eyes were closed. "Interested in sports, Marina?"

"Just thought I'd watch with Harbor," she responded breezily. "Do you . . . have any favorites on these teams? Since Diana Taurasi isn't on them."

Harbor turned, eyes narrowed at Marina. Marina was worried Harbor was going to snap at her, tell her to stop talking, tell her to go away and leave her alone.

Instead, Harbor started rambling. About her favorite team (the Liberty) and her favorite players, and why they were her favorite players. She pointed out certain plays during the game, explaining what was happening. She told Marina what fouls were, and why sometimes the player who got fouled got to shoot twice. She told Marina each basket was worth two points, but that if you shot outside of a certain area, those baskets were so impressive they were worth three.

It was a lot of information in a very short time. Marina understood maybe half of it. Still, she nodded her head like she was supposed to, and she kept her eyes on the game like she was supposed to, and she listened to Harbor like she was supposed to. Harbor seemed to enjoy having an audience, someone to watch with her. None of the other siblings had ever bothered to. Marina couldn't wait to tell Boom about this progress.

In the kitchen, Mama turned off the sink and came to join them in the living room. She sat right next to Marina. She was super close, as if there wasn't an entire sofa worth of space. It annoyed Marina, who scowled and shifted away.

"What, do I smell or something?" Mama said.

Mom opened her eyes to glance over at them.

"No," Marina said.

"So, then, what? You just don't want to sit with me?"

"No."

"Hey, Marina," Mom interjected, "don't be a jerk to your mama. That's uncalled for."

Marina didn't reply. She continued to lean away from Mama, pressing up against the arm of the couch. Her stomach was hurting a bit, her chest getting tense, just like the feeling she'd tried to describe to Lir.

"Are you upset with me about something?" Mama asked, her voice soft. "You've been exceptionally cranky with me, and just me, lately."

She *was* mad at Mama. If she said that, though, Mama would want to know why. And Marina didn't want to tell her.

She didn't know how to explain it. "I was just trying to watch the game with Harbor—that's all. But I'm done now. I'm going to my room."

"Wait a second," Mom started as Marina got up and stormed off.

"It's fine," Mama said. "Just let her go."

Marina shut the door behind her. She didn't slam it—she knew better—but she didn't close it all that quietly, either. Sam, who was sitting on her bed crisscross-applesauce with a book in her hands, looked up. Marina threw herself face-first onto her bed.

"Are you okay?" Sam asked.

"My stomach hurts," Marina mumbled into her pillow.

She avoided Mama the rest of the night.

CHAPTER EIGHT

Mama was packing a cooler. This meant one thing: they were going to the beach. It was full of water bottles and peaches and cherries. She'd also prepared a couple bags with towels for everyone and a book for herself. She added a water bowl for Good Boy, grabbed his leash, and called for Harbor to help her put the beach chairs in the back of the van.

Most of the time, Mom took them across the bay to Tices Shoal in her boat. After docking, they would wade through the water and climb the ladder at the shore. The ladder led them to a road with access to Island Beach State Park. Today, though, Mom was getting ready to take Sam to visit her grandmother. Which was a relief to Marina, because now they would be driving to the beach instead.

"Can I invite Sonny?" Harbor asked, struggling to carry a chair with each arm.

"And Pork!" shrieked Cordelia. "Please!"

Mama quickly counted seats with her eyes closed. "Yes. Fine."

"You sure you can handle all of them alone?" Mom asked.

Mama kissed her. "Of course I can."

"That's right," Mom said. "Super Mama over here."

"It'd be easier if we all just went to the park instead," Marina suggested. "Less for Mama to have to worry about."

"Yes, we know—you love the park," Mom said, pressing a kiss to Marina's head. "But today is one of the very last beach days, so be good for your mama. Sammy Fish, shake a leg! We gotta get going."

Sam came hustling into the kitchen. She leaned into Mama for a hug. Mama kissed her on the head. "Have a nice time with your grandma," Mama said.

Sam's grandma was her only biological relative still alive. She'd had to move to an assisted living home a few years ago, which was why Sam no longer lived with her. Her grandma sometimes had trouble remembering things. It sometimes made Sam sad when she went to see her.

"Tell your grandma I said hi," Harbor said. "I'm gonna take these to the car and go ask Sonny if he can come to the beach."

"Pork too," Lir chimed in.

"If we must go to the beach instead of the park," Marina said, "then can I ask Boom to come, too?"

Mama was shoving extra waters in the cooler. She really

needed a bigger cooler. "We're kind of jammed tight as it is, Marina."

"There's an extra seat in the car, since Mom and Sam aren't coming. If Harbor sits in the front seat," Marina suggested.

Mom had a giant van she said they owned out of necessity. It had two rows of three seats, so it could fit eight people total. It came in handy when it was the entire family plus their bookbags during the school year, or during carpools when Harbor's friends on her basketball team needed rides to practice, or when the five Ali-O'Connor kids wanted to invite their friends to go with them to the beach.

"I really don't like Harbor sitting in the front seat," Mama said.

"Everyone else gets to invite their friends," Marina said. "*I* have a friend now, too!"

Mama pinched the bridge of her nose. "Fine! Okay. Go invite Boom. But make sure her parents know it's just me and an army of children."

Boom's mom did not mind that it was just Mama on supervising duty. In fact, she seemed relieved to get Boom out of the house. The two younger Badger brothers were also allowed to go. The seven kids and Mama, along with the cooler and the beach chairs and Good Boy, all piled into the van. The van had never felt so small. The kids received strict instructions to buckle their seat belts and to sit without wriggling around. (That last bit was directed specifically at Cordelia.) With Harbor in the front, Cordelia, Lir, and Pork in the middle (with Good Boy taking up the extra space by their feet), and Sonny (with the cooler in his lap), Marina, and Boom in the back, off they went to the beach.

They parked the car, and everyone got to work. They proceeded like a parade. Sonny and Harbor carried the chairs, and Mama carried the cooler. Marina and Boom each took a beach bag, while Cordelia, Lir, and Pork carried the umbrella on top of their heads. They found a spot nice and close to the water, but far enough away that if the tide came in, the waves wouldn't wash away their belongings. Good Boy's leash was tied to the cooler, and he tugged on it, trying to get to the water. Sonny helped Mama dig the umbrella deep into the sand so it wouldn't blow away.

"Okay, team, listen up," Mama said. "There are a lot of you and only one of me, so I need you all to do your part to stay safe this trip. Everyone is going to buddy up. Your job is to keep an eye out for your buddy. Sonny, you keep an eye on Pork—"

"And I keep an eye on Sonny?" Pork asked.

Mama smiled at him. "Exactly. Harbor, you've got both Cordelia and Lir. And then Marina and Boom, you two look out for each other. Sound good?"

"Who is Good Boy partnered with?" Cordelia asked.

"How about you look out for Good Boy?" Mama said.

"Who are you looking out for?" Pork asked.

Mama winked. "I've got at least one eye on every single one of you."

It was one of those perfect beach days, sunny with a breeze that kept them from feeling too hot. Mama helped everyone put sunscreen on, especially Harbor, who burned if she so much as thought about the sunlight. And since there were only a few days left before the school year started, a lot of people were on the beach with them. Umbrellas peppered the sand like brightly colored trees in a forest. Families were screeching and splashing in the waves. The lifeguards kept a lookout from their perch, occasionally blowing their whistles if someone swam out too far.

Cordelia buried Mama's toes in the sand, and started to build a sandcastle right on top of them. Pork and Lir looked for the best shells to decorate the castle with. Good Boy lay next to Mama under the shade of the umbrella, whining anytime a seagull dared get too close. Mama filled his bowl with water. Every so often, Good Boy would notice Harbor and Sonny disappear under the waves, and he would jump up, concerned and barking, until they popped back out again.

Lir was in charge of carrying the bucket Pork had filled with shells, since Lir didn't want to touch them until they rinsed them off in the other bucket they had filled with water. Cordelia looked inside. "These shells are *okay*, but we can do better! I want those really pretty scallop ones."

Marina and Boom stood at the edge of the shore, letting the waves lap over their feet and watching them sink into the wet sand.

"Where's your phone?" Marina asked. "I'm surprised you're not filming. Sometimes we see dolphins here."

"I'm too busy looking at it. It's so *big*." Boom waved her hands, gesturing at the Atlantic Ocean.

"Did you know we've only ever explored like twenty percent of the ocean?" Marina said. "There's so much out there we don't even know. Like, right underneath Sonny and Harbor. We know nothing."

"That's scary," Boom said.

Marina wholeheartedly agreed.

And then a wave crashed against the shore, and Boom reached out and pushed Marina right into it.

The water rushed over Marina's head, and she flopped on the hard, damp sand, momentarily stunned like a beached whale. She pushed her hair out of her face, pulled a strand of seagrass from her now-floppy giant bun, and glared at Boom.

Boom was downright cackling.

"That was uncalled for!" yelled Marina.

"Exposure therapy!" said Boom between bouts of laughter. "I read all about it. It's a way to face your fear by being, well, *pushed* right into it."

"Yeah, well, it didn't work!"

"You should see your face right now. Stay there. I'm coming in!"

Boom ran directly at Marina. Marina tried to scramble to her feet, but a wave came behind her and knocked her down again. Boom reached for Marina's arms and pulled her to standing.

They caught up to Sonny and Harbor, who were deeper in the water, bodysurfing in the waves. Harbor looked confused when she saw Marina. Marina opened her mouth to speak, but she didn't get the chance to. Another wave knocked into her head. She came out the other side, sputtering seawater.

Sonny laughed. "Do you guys want to play a game? Maybe we can have a race to see who can bodysurf to shore fastest."

"Yes! Let's do it!" boomed Boom.

Marina wasn't exactly thrilled by the game, but she lined up with the four of them, waiting for the perfect wave. "Here comes a good one!" called Harbor as they watched it build in the distance, growing and funneling as it came closer and closer. "Everybody ready? Wait for it . . . and . . . *go!*"

Marina couldn't remember the last time she'd gone swimming in the ocean. She didn't think she'd stepped foot in it at all this summer. She kicked her feet, quickly, quickly, quickly. She felt the wave start to push her, and she didn't like that feeling—it made her stomach hurt. She moved her arms and legs faster, trying to keep up with everyone else. The wave picked her up, she swam as hard as she could, and suddenly she was going fast. Too fast.

Really, *really* fast.

She squealed as the wave carried her along, speeding past Sonny and Boom—and Harbor, too. She crashed with the wave against the sand. It sent her spiraling, rolling around and around and *around*, until she finally came to a stop. Her chest heaved as she lay on the ground, staring up at the sky and the sun, trying to catch her breath.

Three shadows fell over her as the heads of Harbor, Sonny, and Boom came into view.

"Whoa. Are you okay?"

"Are you hurt?"

"Should I get Mama?"

All at once, a big wet slobbering tongue was licking her face, and the lifeguards were blowing their whistles. Good Boy had escaped from his confines and no one was holding on to his leash. Harbor reached to grab it, pulling him off Marina. "Let her breathe, you big lug."

Marina gulped in air. "I definitely just won."

"Oh yeah. You definitely won," Sonny said.

Harbor rolled her eyes. She turned to give a thumbs-up to Mama, who had been watching the whole ordeal. "She's fine."

Marina sat up and brushed the sand out of her hair. She immediately realized this would be an impossible task. "I think

I'll sit the next one out," she said. "I'll be the judge instead."

The other three waited approximately two seconds to make sure Marina was positive before they took off, back into the water. Marina stood up, shaking the clumped wet sand out of her bathing suit the best she could. She took Good Boy's leash and tugged him along with her as she made her way back to Mama and the beach chairs. She flopped down into one. Pork immediately started burying her feet. Mama tied Good Boy's leash more securely, this time to her own chair.

"You okay, sweetheart?" Mama asked. "That looked rough."

Marina nodded. "I'm fine, but that was enough ocean for me for one day, I'm pretty sure."

Mama had nearly an entire castle on top of her feet. It had three walls and two stories, and was liberally decorated with seashells. Pork and Lir were using their biggest bucket to build the first part of the new castle on top of Marina's feet. Marina wiggled her toes, and it came tumbling right down. "It's a dragon!" exclaimed Lir. "Terrorizing our castle!"

"Roar," Marina said. "Get away from my feet."

Lir and Pork went back to Mama's feet.

Marina watched them add to Mama's foot castle. She turned around and saw Good Boy, dozing in the sun. She kept turning, glancing toward the water, where Sonny, Harbor, and Boom were bobbing in the waves. She made another full circle before saying, "Where's Cordelia?"

Mama moved so quickly that the sandcastle immediately came down. She made the exact same circle Marina had. "She was just here . . . Lir, where's your sister?"

"She went looking for seashells," Pork said.

"*Where?*" Mama said.

Lir looked around, too. "Um . . ."

Cordelia often wandered. She wandered in the grocery store (usually to go look at the live lobsters). She wandered in school (she'd get distracted and somehow end up in a different direction than the rest of her class). Apparently, she wandered at the beach also.

"You were supposed to have one eye on everyone," Marina yelled at Mama. Her stomach was hurting again. She was breathing super quickly, too.

"That's not helpful, Marina," Mama scolded. Then she called out, "Cordelia!"

Lir called her name, too.

Harbor must have spotted the look on Mama's face. She came jogging over, with Sonny and Boom at her heels. "What's wrong?"

"Go tell the lifeguard Cordelia is missing. She's wearing her green bathing suit, I think. Right? Or was it the yellow one?" Mama shook her head.

"You were supposed to be the twins' buddy," Marina said to Harbor.

"But I was—"

"Just *go*, Harbor!" snapped Mama.

Harbor took off running for the lifeguard stand. Mama took Lir and Pork by the arms, sitting them down on the towel. "You two sit right here and do not move. Understood? Do not move from this spot."

They both nodded.

Two of the lifeguards came jogging over with Harbor and Sonny. Mama immediately explained to them that Cordelia was missing, that she was just right here and now she wasn't, and she couldn't see her anywhere. One of the lifeguards started running down by the water, searching. Mama kept calling out Cordelia's name, and Harbor reached out to hold her hand. The other lifeguard recapped the situation over his walkie-talkie. Good Boy was barking his head off. Sonny tried to calm him down while also comforting Pork, who had started crying. Boom, falling quieter than Marina had ever seen her, sat down next to Lir.

Marina was having trouble breathing.

She felt like she had when the wave had picked her up and spun her out of control. When the water had rushed over her head and sent her spiraling hard onto the sand. She couldn't suck in a good breath. It felt like something was pressing hard against her throat. She placed a hand on top of her chest, trying to feel for whatever was blocking the air from getting from her lungs to where it needed to be.

Her eyes burned.

That was when Marina saw her: the small figure in the green tankini (Mama had been right) standing far away, next to the fishermen who had their giant poles stuck into the sand like Mama's umbrella. Marina tried to open her mouth and say, *There! She's over there!* But she couldn't. She couldn't breathe, and she couldn't talk, and Cordelia was right over there. Marina reached for whoever was closest to her—Harbor—and grabbed her arm as tightly as she could. Once she had Harbor's attention, she pointed a finger in Cordelia's direction.

"Mama! There she is!" said Harbor.

Mama and Harbor took off running. Mama grabbed Cordelia and pulled her up and into her arms, even though Cordelia was getting much too big to be carried. Mama thanked the lifeguards and everyone else who had helped.

When she got back to the group, Mama alternated between hugging and reprimanding Cordelia. The rest of the kids stayed quiet, not really sure what to do, now that the immediate danger was over.

Marina still couldn't breathe.

She buried her face in her hands and started crying. Boom noticed right away. "Marina? Are you okay?" Marina didn't answer her. Her stomach still hurt, and she still couldn't breathe, and now she also couldn't stop crying.

"Marina says sometimes her chest gets super tight and it's too hard to breathe the right way," Lir said quietly. "Maybe that's what's happening now."

Suddenly, Mama was kneeling down in front of her. She gently pulled Marina's hands away from her face. She pushed Marina's hair out of her eyes, and cupped Marina's cheek.

"I can't breathe," Marina choked out.

Mama tugged her closer. "Cordelia is safe. You're safe, too. Everyone's okay."

"I can't breathe, Mama!"

"Shh. Hey, look at me. Everyone is okay. You are, too. You got scared, and that's all right. Let your body catch up to your head." Mama took Marina's hand and placed it on her own chest. "Follow me, okay? Breathe in." Mama breathed deeply in. "Breathe out." She breathed out. "Try it with me, okay?"

Marina nodded.

"Breathe in."

Marina took a stuttering breath in.

"Breathe out."

She let the air back out again.

"Breathe in."

Marina breathed in.

"Breathe out."

Marina breathed back out again.

They did that a couple more times, until Marina was able to breathe alone again. Mama held her close, and Marina let her. She leaned into Mama, until a Frisbee landed nearby and Marina remembered where they were. She pulled away, embarrassed, avoiding eye contact with anyone. Especially Harbor. Especially Boom.

"Okay. I think it's time we called it," Mama said. "Everyone help me pack up so we can go home."

Mama kept a comforting hand on Marina's back, and a *You'd best not leave my side again* hand on Cordelia's arm. Everyone quickly and quietly shook the sand off the towels. Sonny took down the umbrella, and Harbor folded up the beach chairs. They followed Mama like a row of baby ducklings, with Harbor at the rear keeping watch, as they walked through the sand up the beach to the car.

No one said anything the entire drive home.

CHAPTER NINE

After the mess at the beach, Marina was all set to abandon her and Boom's plans. If Mama couldn't always be Cordelia's safety net even though Cordelia was one of Mama's favorites, what hope was there for Marina? Honestly, there was no point. Marina thought her time would be much better spent crawling into bed and remaining under the covers for the rest of summer. And maybe even longer after that.

Boom did not agree. In Boom's opinion, a crowded beach and a wandering sister was an exception to the rule. Mama could keep up with only so many of them at once, and Boom was skeptical that she would ever volunteer to take everyone to the beach without Mom as *her* safety net ever again.

Marina had to admit Boom was probably right about that part.

They did not speak about Marina's trouble breathing. Marina was glad. She didn't like everyone knowing she was a giant scaredy-cat. The last thing she wanted was to talk about it. She'd been avoiding being alone with her moms for the same reason.

"Do you have good running shoes?" Boom asked when she came over the day after the beach, her phone battery charged to one hundred percent.

"I have my gym sneakers," Marina said. "Does that count?"

"Go ask Harbor if she'll play basketball with you. But wait—let me get it on camera." Boom fiddled with the settings on her phone. "Okay, I'm ready."

"The last thing Harbor is going to want to do is play basketball with me," Marina said, with Boom's phone pointing at her face. "I am terrible at basketball. Can't I just keep watching games with her instead?"

"Do any of your siblings ever offer to play basketball with Harbor?"

"No."

"You need to be the one to do it if you want to bump into favorite-sister territory, then."

"Ugh. *Fine.*"

When Marina and Boom approached Harbor, she was doing her summer reading. She hadn't started yet, which Mom had been particularly angry about. Harbor was basically in time-out. She wasn't allowed to go hang with Sonny unless she'd at least read a little bit. She stared at Marina and Boom, and Marina could tell she was ready to yell at them to leave her alone. Harbor turned the page so aggressively it ripped a little.

Boom elbowed Marina.

"Do . . . do you want to play basketball?" she asked.

Harbor stared at her, blinking. "*You* want to play basketball?"

"Um. If you want to."

Harbor was looking at the two of them like they had merged bodies or grown extra heads or something.

Marina didn't really blame her. She thought Harbor would still tell them to go away and leave her alone.

But then Harbor said, "Let me just finish this chapter."

It took Harbor longer than Marina thought it would, but then she slammed the book shut, got her basketball out of the garage, and laced up her very favorite bright-orange Candace Parker Adidas sneakers. When Harbor first began playing basketball, her dad bought her a brand-new hoop, which he installed in his driveway. At the time, their moms couldn't afford a nice one like that. Theirs was rusty and old. It wasn't cemented into the driveway. It was weighed down, but when it got really windy, like during a hurricane or tropical storm, it'd blow up the street or completely fall over.

"If we play Twenty-One or something, it'll be boring, because you'll lose," Harbor said. Marina didn't take offense to this. It was certainly true. "So I was thinking, maybe we play Horse."

"Okay," Marina said. "How do you play Horse?"

Harbor sighed, apparently burdened with having to teach Marina everything. "We take turns taking shots. But you can take any sort of shot you want. It could be easy, like a foul shot . . ."

Marina silently questioned Harbor's definition of *easy*.

"Or super hard, like making a basket while standing backward or something. If you make the shot, the other person has to do it the exact same way. If they make it, it's their turn to make up a shot. If they miss, they get a letter. Once someone spells 'horse,' they lose."

Boom was sitting on the curb, filming them. "This is going to be a very short game, isn't it?" she asked.

Marina stuck her tongue out at her. But she was probably right.

"Here. You can go first," Harbor said. It was the nicest thing Harbor had probably said to her the entire summer, so Marina had to admit they were off to a good start.

Marina took the orange-and-white WNBA ball. It felt big and heavy in her hands, and she spread her feet wider so she felt more balanced. She stood there for a moment, staring at the hoop in front of her. It was so tall she had to crane her neck.

"Try something fun," Boom said.

"Like what?"

"Bounce it really, really hard and see if you can get it to go in!"

That seemed highly unlikely. When Marina dared a glance at Harbor, however, she looked really excited at the idea.

Marina took a couple steps back, eyeing the basket warily. She bounced the ball a couple of times—with both her hands at once, which Harbor immediately told her not to do—just to see how it felt.

"Do it as hard as you can," Boom said.

Marina took a deep breath, held the ball above her head as high as she possibly could, and slammed it down with all her strength. It bounced off the street and flew up into the air. Marina watched with wide eyes as it brushed against the bottom of the net and fell onto the rocks that were scattered around their front lawn.

"Oh my god, that was so close!" Harbor said. She ran to collect the ball and then came to stand exactly where Marina was standing, bumping her aside with her hip. "Let me try!"

Harbor did exactly the same thing as Marina. She lifted the ball high above her head and, in one swift movement, slammed it to the ground. The ball hit and bounced high, high, high. Marina thought it would definitely go in.

It didn't. It hit the net and airballed, just like Marina's did, though Harbor's was a little closer.

But Harbor didn't look disappointed by the miss. In fact, she was smiling. "Okay, new game," Harbor said. "First one to bounce the ball into the basket wins."

Harbor and Marina took turns. Each time one of them lined up a shot, they all counted down: "Three, two, one!" Then the ball was slammed as hard as possible into the ground, scaring the seagulls perched on the neighboring houses. It didn't take long before Boom put her phone away and got up to try, too.

On one of Marina's turns, she jumped at the same time she threw the ball to the ground. It went higher than any other shot had and bounced off the rim.

"That was the closest yet!" Harbor said. "Don't move. You have to try again!"

Even though it was Harbor's turn, she handed the ball back to Marina.

Boom gave Marina an enthusiastic wink.

Holy cow, this is working! Marina thought. Sam, Cordelia, and Lir *never* played basketball with Harbor. Even Sonny Badger, who was Harbor's best friend, preferred baseball.

Maybe Harbor would be her safety net.

Marina lined the ball up again. She was determined to make this shot. If she could just make this shot, she thought, it would seal the deal.

She could do this. She *could*.

"Three!" shouted Boom, her phone back out as she filmed Marina.

Harbor joined in. "Two!"

"One!" all three of them yelled.

Marina bounced the ball with every single bit of strength she had. She tried harder than she had ever tried to do anything before. It hit the ground and flew into the air, higher,

higher, higher. She held her breath as she watched it soar. It was going to go in. It really was!

It hit the backboard, and Marina thought, *Oh my gosh, this is it! It's going to fall right in!*

But suddenly, there was a loud *crack*. The backboard was coming loose. It swung down and sent the ball crashing to earth, where it bounced and rolled away.

Harbor gasped. The backboard continued swinging there, back and forth, back and forth, as they all stood frozen watching it.

And then . . . it fell.

The backboard hit the ground with an echoing *bang*, squashing the net underneath it.

The three of them didn't move.

Harbor started clenching her jaw, which was something everyone knew she did when she was trying not to cry.

"Harbor . . ." Marina said, reaching out to touch her arm.

Harbor jerked away. She clenched her jaw even harder, and Marina knew it was only a matter of time before—

"*Moooooom!*" screamed Harbor, stretching the word out to one long wail.

Marina still didn't move. Boom grabbed her arm and tugged at her. "Let's go!" said Boom, and the two of them ran as quickly as they could into the house to hide. Whether or not it was actually Marina's fault didn't matter. She knew with certainty that Harbor wasn't going to let this one go for a while.

Which meant that Marina had exactly zero chance of becoming Harbor's favorite by Labor Day weekend.

Late that afternoon, a summer storm came blowing through the neighborhood. The sky had been blue one minute and angry, swirling dark grays the next. Good Boy was the first to alert the family to the storm. He had been hiding in the bathroom about a half hour before it actually began. He always seemed to sense these things before anyone else. Lir said it was because he had excellent ultrasonic hearing.

They'd quickly brought their belongings inside. Mama even managed to bring the smaller outdoor furniture to safety, so it wouldn't get blown into the lagoon and float away. Getting the house ready for the spontaneous storm took no time at all. That wasn't the issue. The issue was that *Harbor Me* wasn't tied up and secure along their dock. Instead, it was out on the bay somewhere with Mom, Mr. Martin, and Mr. Harris. They'd left early that morning to go fishing, and hadn't come home yet.

When they went on their big fishing expeditions, they were usually out until after dark. But as the sun set and the storm kept rolling, Marina's stomach hurt so bad she couldn't eat dinner. Mama told the kids Mom had texted that she was going to try and find somewhere to dock. Mama assured them Mom knew what she was doing, that she was the best boater, and that she would be home soon.

Bedtime came, and Mom still wasn't home. Marina couldn't sleep. She stared at Diana Taurasi, and Diana Taurasi stared back before Marina gave in, said "Good night," and closed her eyes tight. When she opened them and looked at her clock, she realized it was an entire hour later. She must have fallen asleep for a little bit. Maybe Mom had gotten home while she'd slept. She climbed out of bed and quietly made her way out of the bedroom, careful not to wake Sam or Harbor. Harbor, especially, hated being woken up by anybody.

Across the hall, Marina could see the light from under her moms' bedroom door, which meant, at the very least, someone was still awake. It made her think that Mom must have gotten home and was telling Mama all about her day before they'd turn off the light and go to bed, too. She hurried over, knocked gently and quickly, and then swung the door open.

Inside, Mama was lying on her side of the bed. She was under the covers with a book in her lap. A quick scan of the bedroom showed no sight of Mom. "Hey, sweetheart," Mama said. "Everything all right?"

"Is Mom home?"

Mama shook her head. "Not yet. She was texting me a little while ago, though. She's okay. They had to dock pretty far away for a bit, to wait out the worst of it. Now they're just trying to get home as fast as they can."

Marina shifted her weight from one foot to the other as she hovered by the door. "Are you waiting up for her?"

"I am," Mama said. "Do you want to join me?"

Marina exhaled very deeply. "Yes," she said.

Mama pulled down the comforter on Mom's side of the bed, patting the empty spot. Marina jumped in, and Mama wrapped an arm around her, keeping her closer than she needed to in such a large bed. Marina had that familiar feeling, the one that made her want to pull away from Mama. But her chest was really tight, and she remembered what it was like to feel Mama's deep breaths on the beach. So, instead of moving away, Marina got closer, resting her head against Mama's chest. With each breath Mama took, Marina felt like she was being rocked by soft waves in the ocean.

"You worry about everyone a lot, don't you, Marina?" Mama said as she ran her fingers through Marina's hair. She was careful not to tug the knots, gently untangling them instead.

"There are over two *thousand* boating injuries each year," Marina said, "and Mom goes out on her boat a lot."

"That's a scary statistic," Mama said.

"Yes," Marina breathed. "Very."

Mama kept brushing her fingers through Marina's hair. "Mom will be home soon. I promise. Try and relax and close your eyes."

Marina did as her mama told her. Within minutes, she fell asleep.

CHAPTER TEN

Without her sound machine blocking out the noise, Marina could hear Good Boy whining to go out. She heard the *clackety-clack* of his nails on the hardwood floor as he paced. The sound made Marina think that he needed to get his nails filed, and he could probably use a grooming, too. For a short-haired dog, he sure shed pretty often.

Marina opened her eyes to see what time it was. She grew confused when she didn't see her alarm clock right in front of her. When she looked up at the wall, Diana Taurasi wasn't staring down at her. Instead, she saw a black-and-white photo from the beach. It was the first family picture of the entire Ali-O'Connor family together. Mom had asked a stranger sitting under an umbrella to take it. It had turned out so well Mama had sent it away to be printed extra-large for them to frame and hang on their bedroom wall.

Oh, right. Marina wasn't in her bedroom. She was in her moms'.

She rolled over and came face-to-face with Mom. Mom was lying on her side, and she scooted even closer, pressing her forehead against Marina's. "Hey, little fish," she said. "I heard you were worried about me last night."

Marina didn't waste a single second. She barrel-hugged Mom around the middle, holding her super-super-tight. Mom held her just as tightly back.

Mom shifted so she was sitting up, with Marina tucked into her lap.

"Was it awful?" Marina asked her. "Were you scared?"

"You know how I have all my boating rules? The safety rules that I make us go over before we go out on the boats? Why we made Sam wear a life vest any time she was on the dock until we were sure she could swim? Still do, when there's no one outside with her?" Mom said. "Well, when me and Mr. Martin and Mr. Harris go out on long fishing trips, we plan. We prepare. Sometimes unexpected things happen, like big scary storms. But we try to be ready for anything. That's why all the rules. That's why I teach you and your siblings everything I do."

"Accidents happen, though," Marina said. "Boats sink. Or capsize. Or get attacked by pirates."

"I can honestly say I have not heard about a single pirate attack in Barnegat Bay for as long as I've been boating here. But I do suppose there is a first time for everything," Mom said.

"Exactly!"

"Mama also told me you had a bit of a panic attack when Cordelia wandered on the beach. You had trouble breathing, right?"

Marina scowled. "Mama should mind her own business."

Mom sighed. "You've been exceptionally hard on your mama lately, you know? It makes her sad. It makes me sad, too. Do you want to tell me what that's about?"

"No. I don't know," Marina said. She could hear Cordelia and Lir running down the hall toward the kitchen. Cordelia was shouting about wanting pancakes. Good Boy, who must have been back from his walk, started barking his head off. This was how the morning in the Ali-O'Connor house usually began. Loudly, all at once, and right away.

"Can I go now? Can I just go eat breakfast before Cordelia makes a super mess with the syrup? I hate when the table is all sticky and she gets it all over everything, and I like my pancakes dry anyway, and—"

"This is important, my little fish. You used to love coming on the boats with me. I have the best memories of you as a baby in a tiny life jacket that still seemed way too big, sitting with Mama right next to me while I drove. I miss that. I miss *you* this summer, and I hate that you keep missing out on these big family things," Mom said. "Like the Fourth of July."

"I had a really good time that day at Mr. Martin's!"

"We need to talk about this, Marina."

"We don't. Mom, no, we don't," Marina said. She didn't want to talk about this. Just thinking about talking about all the things she felt—about the boats and Mama and everyone—made her stomach hurt all over again. "I'll come on the boat for the Parade of Lights. I promise. Okay? Then you'll see it's fine. I'm fine. Right?"

"Marina—"

"I promise, okay? I'll come on the boat for the Parade of Lights. Can I please go eat breakfast now?"

Mom hesitated, watching Marina carefully. But then she sighed. "Fine. Okay. Go get something to eat."

Marina climbed out of the bed and left the room before Mom could change her mind.

This was bad. This was very, very bad. When an Ali-O'Connor made a promise, they were supposed to keep it. No matter what. When Harbor promised her dad she would spend her birthday with him, she did. Even though she'd cried the whole day before, because she didn't want to spend her birthday away from home. Sam promised her grandma that she would visit her in the assisted living home as much as she could. Even though she sometimes dreaded those visits, because sometimes her grandma couldn't remember Sam, and it made Sam sad, she always went. Even though their moms told her if she really didn't want to, that was okay.

Mom always promised Mama she would call her if she was going to be home late. Once, she didn't, and they had a big fight about it. Mom made sure to call every single time since.

Marina had foolishly promised Mom she would be on the boat for the Parade of Lights. She was lamenting this fact to Boom, who was recording it on camera. "We better get a move on things, then," Boom said. "You should sleep over tonight so we can really strategize."

Marina had never slept over at anyone's house before. She liked her bed, and her sound machine, and sleep. Three things that she definitely wouldn't have at Boom's house. "I don't know . . ." Marina said. She started to explain all the reasons why she probably shouldn't.

Boom's face fell.

Marina backtracked a bit. "Well, maybe you can sleep here instead."

Marina had never had anyone sleep over before, either. Harbor had, though, and it was fine, she supposed.

Boom smiled very big. "Okay!"

"I have to ask my mom first."

"Okay! Great! Go ask her!"

"Now?"

"Yes, Marina! Go ask now!"

Marina thought that maybe she'd get lucky and Mom would say no, but she said yes so quickly Marina's head spun a little bit. Boom wasted no time, darting across the street to ask her mom for permission. She came back barely ten minutes later with a packed backpack and a sleeping bag.

Not only would it be the first time Boom slept over at the Ali-O'Connors', but she would be staying for dinner, too. Mom added another folding chair to the table. She let Boom sit in her usual spot, next to Marina, while she sat across the way, next to Lir. Mom barbecued chicken legs, and Lir showed Boom how to wrap a napkin around the bone part so you didn't have to get chicken juice and barbecue sauce all over your hand while you ate it. Cordelia spent a good fifteen minutes explaining to Boom all the types of legs besides chicken legs you could eat if you wanted. "Frog legs. Lamb legs. Mom, can you eat cow legs?"

"Beef shanks," Mom answered.

"Beef shanks!"

"My mom would hate this conversation," Boom said with glee. "She's a vegetarian."

Good Boy, with his scavenger instincts, targeted the new presence at the table. He sat big and tall next to Boom the entire dinner, waiting patiently. His patience was rewarded when Boom thought no one was looking (Marina was) and casually dropped him a piece of chicken. He gobbled it up and then knocked into the table as he went under it, causing everyone to hold on like there was an earthquake. Then he made his way to Cordelia's feet to lick up her crumbs.

After dinner, Boom offered to help wash the dishes. Which meant Marina would also have to help wash the dishes. Boom stood between Mama and Marina as they made an assembly line. Mama would wash, Boom would rinse, and Marina would dry.

"So where did you move here from, Boom?" Mama asked.

"Not far. In Middletown? We moved here because the taxes were cheaper and my dad likes the water," Boom explained.

Mama laughed. "I haven't met your dad yet," she said.

"Oh, he's not here. He'll be gone for a while. He's a cameraman, and he's on a big crab boat in Alaska right now. He's filming them for the Discovery Channel."

Marina blinked. She hadn't known that.

"You must miss him," Mama said.

"Yeah. I guess." Boom handed three dishes at once to Marina to dry. "Hey, I've got a joke. What kind of exercise do dishes do?"

"What?" Mama said.

"*Puh-lay-tees!*"

"That was awful!" called Mom from the other room, but Mama kept laughing.

Marina quickly dried the last of the three dishes and then tugged at Boom so they could finally leave the kitchen. The last thing Marina needed was Boom making Mama laugh, making Mama like her a lot.

As they brushed their teeth together, with the bathroom door closed for privacy, Boom got down to business. "So . . . tell me about Sam. I tried to watch her during dinner, but

I couldn't learn much. She sort of just ate her food like normal."

Sam was next up on their safety-net list. While Marina was relieved Sam had no interest in sports, the only thing she *did* have an interest in was Mom's business, which meant boats. Which didn't exactly help Marina, since her fear of boats was the reason they were doing all of this to begin with.

"That's Sam," Marina said. "She's probably the best behaved out of all of us."

"Who's her favorite?"

Marina paused to think. "Mom, maybe? I know Harbor is probably her least favorite. They fight a lot."

"Well, you know she'd have your back over Harbor's, at least."

"True."

There was a knock on the bathroom door. "Hurry up!" yelled Harbor.

They ignored her.

"What does Sam like best? We were doing so well with basketball and Harbor until the whole thing fell apart," Boom said. "Can we just do the same thing but with Sam?"

Marina sighed and turned off the sink. "Sam likes boats. And I am not playing Horse games anywhere near a boat."

"Hmm," Boom said.

When they'd finished washing up, Marina set up Boom's sleeping bag on the floor while apologizing for the mess of her shared bedroom. Boom would be lying right next to Marina's bed. She would have to make sure to remember to climb out the other side if she had to go to the bathroom in the middle of the night.

Boom pointed at Harbor's poster. "Whoa, she looks awesome. Who is she?"

"That's Diana Taurasi," Marina said. "Make sure you say good night to her, so she doesn't wake up in the middle of the night to bounce a basketball on your head."

Sam, who was climbing into her own bed, said, "She does *what*?"

"I say good night to her every night, Sam, and you should start, too."

Sam looked at Marina, then up at the poster, then back at Marina, then up at the poster again. "Good night," she said.

Harbor was having a tantrum in the living room, arguing with their moms, so it was just the three of them in the bedroom. They could hear Harbor getting herself more and more worked up.

"What's got her goat?" Boom asked.

"She wants to be able to have a sleepover with Sonny, but she's not allowed," Sam explained.

"She gets super upset at the end of the summer, because the Badger brothers go back home for school. They leave next week," Marina explained.

"Why can't she have a sleepover with him?" Boom asked.

"Because he's a boy," Marina said.

"But your moms are gay!" exclaimed Boom.

"Our moms are fine with it," Marina said. "Sonny's grandma is not. She's old-school."

"Interesting," Boom said. She gave Marina a really big, obvious wink. She turned around in her sleeping bag to face Sam. "So, what about you?"

"What about me?" Sam asked.

"Marina has me. Harbor has Sonny. The twins have Pork Chop." Boom was counting out on her fingers. "Who's your best friend?"

Sam got really, really quiet. It made Marina's stomach hurt.

"I have some friends at school," Sam finally said.

"But not here?" pushed Boom.

Marina wanted to tell her to stop.

She didn't, though, so Boom continued: "Well, good thing you have a bunch of siblings, right? Like Marina, right? Especially since you're both adopted. You must have a lot in common."

"Yeah," Sam said softly. "I guess."

Boom tucked her hands under her head, eyes pointed to the ceiling. "I don't have any siblings. It must be so cool to have so many."

It was then that Harbor pushed the door open—hard—slamming it against the wall in a way that had Mom calling, "Harbor! Watch it!" from down the hall. She turned off the overhead light and flopped into her bed, giving everyone strict orders to "Be quiet and go to sleep."

Boom, after a few moments, glanced up at Marina and whispered, "Or maybe not." Though because it was Boom, it wasn't quite a whisper. Marina laughed.

Mom, and then Mama, both popped their heads in to say good night. Marina turned on her sound machine and was relieved when Boom didn't comment on it.

"Good night," Boom said, and then added much louder: "And good night to you, too, awesome basketball lady on Harbor's poster!"

CHAPTER ELEVEN

In the morning, Mama made waffles. Boom ate three.

Sam escaped pretty quickly after eating only half of one. She went to the shed to grab her small fishing rod. There were little fish jumping in the bay. She tried to get Mom to fish with her, but Mom had to go work at Joe Koch's marina for the day. Mom kissed everyone on the head, including Boom, and gave Mama a peck on the lips before leaving.

Sam went outside alone.

Boom noticed immediately. She elbowed Marina between syrup-covered bites of her third waffle. "Now's your chance, you know. She's bummed your mom couldn't fish with her. So you gotta weasel your way in. Let me finish this bite, and we can go outside, too."

"Maybe we should leave Sam alone. We can just go to the park instead. You missed it, but Sam had kind of a bad summer. She and George Badger crashed a boat," Marina explained. Sam had been trying to prove to George that she could drive a boat, and they'd made some terrible decisions. George was still grounded, as far as Marina knew. She hadn't seen much of him since.

Remembering all of that reminded Marina of something very important. "Actually, Sam *just* learned how to swim, you know. She's not even that great at it yet. So I don't know how great a safety net she'll be anyway, even if I *was* her favorite. She'd be too busy needing a safety net herself. She barely managed to keep her head above water when she was in that boat crash."

Boom relinquished the last bite of her waffle to Good Boy, who had been eagerly waiting for it. "Well, you know, lightning doesn't strike the same place twice—"

"I don't think that's actually true—"

"So if Sam already had a boat crash this summer, what are the odds anything that bad would happen to her again? So maybe Sam is the family member you should stick closest to," Boom said. She wiped off her hands and got up to put her plate in the sink. "Come on. We'll go test her."

"We'll do what?"

"See how good her swimming skills are, to see if she would make a good safety net."

Sam, as usual, wasn't having any luck catching fish, but it didn't stop her from continuing to try. Her legs were dangling off the dock as she flung her line into the water. Marina wanted to tell her to scoot back a little so she wouldn't fall in. Boom stood above Sam, leaning over, casting a giant shadow in the lagoon. Sam glanced up at her warily.

"Do you want to go swimming?" Boom asked.

"With you guys?" Sam said.

"Well, actually . . ." Marina said. She was about to explain exactly why *she* didn't want to go into the dark, probably dirty water.

"Yep!" said Boom loudly. "Let's all go swimming!"

So the three of them got their bathing suits on and alerted Mama, who would be watching them from the windows while she finished cleaning up breakfast. Cordelia and Lir wanted to come, too, but Mama told them to wait until she could join them. Boom leaned her camera against the pilings and hit RECORD. Like a proper Sunrise Lagoon kid, she jumped into the water without any hesitation. Sam was still slow to enter. A couple of minutes later, she was still clinging on to the ladder that went from their deck.

"Are you coming?" Boom asked her, eyes narrowed.

"Yeah. I'm just easing in," Sam replied.

"Have you ever just jumped into the lagoon?" Boom asked. "Like, what if you were being chased by that disgusting crab monster over there or something? Would you jump then?"

"Frankencrab isn't gonna chase me anywhere. And I can jump. I've jumped."

Boom swam up to the ladder. "Let's all jump. We can judge who jumps the best."

Sam didn't look all that sure about this new plan. In fairness, neither was Marina, who didn't even want to swim in the lagoon, let alone jump into it. Still, somehow, the three of them ended up lined up along the deck, toes over the edge, staring down into the water.

"What are you guys doing?" It was Sonny Badger calling over from across the way on his grandparents' dock.

"Pretending we have to jump into the water to save our lives from a crab monster," Boom responded.

"Oh? Okay. Can I jump, too?"

"On the count of three, Sonny Badger," Boom said. She reached for Marina's hand. In her biggest, loudest voice, she counted them down. *"Three! Two! One!"*

They all leapt in at once. (Well, Marina mostly got tugged in. She had hesitated, but Boom had been holding her hand.) Bubbles surrounded them as they hit the water and gravity pulled them down. As they kick, kick, kicked to the surface, even more bubbles appeared. Sonny was the first to get his head above the water. Boom was second. She pulled at Marina's arm, helping her up, too. Marina, feeling a little out of control, was flailing around a bit wildly. She accidentally kicked someone before she got above the surface, too.

As Marina shook her damp hair out of her face, Sam popped up, coughing. She must have swallowed some water.

"Sam? Are you okay?" Sonny said.

She kept coughing, so he swam right to her, wrapped his arms around her, and helped get her to the ladder.

The twins, Mama, and Good Boy appeared on the deck. "You drowning?" Cordelia asked.

"Sam, everything okay?" Mama said.

Sam's face was bright red as she clung to the ladder. She was still coughing, but not as much, and she managed to say, "I'm *fine*."

"You might want to practice a bit more," Boom said.

Sam wiped roughly at her eyes. "Someone kicked me. I was fine. I can swim *fine*."

Mama reached toward the ladder with a towel. Sam climbed out, Sonny right behind her. Mama wrapped Sam up and rubbed her back while Sam got control of the coughing.

Sonny turned around to face Marina and Boom in the water.

"I think I accidentally kicked her," Marina admitted.

Sonny made sure Sam and Mama were far enough away not to hear him before he said, "She just learned, you know? So you need to be careful."

Marina nodded, then started swimming toward the ladder.

"Well, you're clearly right," Boom told Marina as she followed. "Sam needs a safety net of her own. So we'll have to move on to the next person on our list."

Marina grabbed a towel. Mama had brought a stack outside for everyone.

Sam was sitting next to Mama on the deck as Cordelia and Lir got ready to go into the water. Sam's face was still pink.

Marina was already running out of siblings. At least, running out of siblings big enough to provide a decent safety net. She was pretty sure, if she was a cat on a roof like in Boom's example, both Lir and Cordelia would get squashed if she jumped to them.

But as Marina watched Sonny Badger kick at the little rocks that spilled over into the driveway, waiting for Harbor and Sam to come outside, Marina realized a very important thing: Sonny Badger was the closest thing she had to an older brother. And older brothers, she figured, would make very good safety nets.

Well, okay, maybe not someone like George, who had proved he absolutely would not be a good safety net when he and Sam got themselves into danger earlier in the summer. But Sonny was not like George. Sonny was the kind of kid who came over to make pancakes and gave Marina extra chocolate chips melted on top of hers because he knew she didn't like dry pancakes but also didn't like syrup. He was the kind of kid who was thoughtful enough to tell Marina and Boom to be careful with Sam, who was still a new swimmer.

He was the kind of kid who would be a safety net if needed.

Marina threw open the front door. Sonny looked up, but when he realized she was neither Harbor nor Sam, he kicked at another rock and ignored her.

"Sonny Badger," Marina said.

"Yeah?"

That was as far as Marina got before she realized she didn't even really know what she was going to say. Sonny liked baseball (but Marina had done enough sports bonding attempts, thank you very much) and cooking (Marina did not want to be anywhere near a hot oven or stove—that sounded like an accident waiting to happen). There wasn't much else to bond with him over.

He was only two years older than her, though, and he was best friends with Harbor and really good friends with Sam. Maybe Marina just needed to be his friend, too. Maybe if she just hung out with him like they did, he'd automatically be her safety net.

"We should hang out more," Marina said.

"Oh?" Sonny got very still, his foot freezing in midair instead of kicking the rock he had been about to kick.

"Yes. I think we should spend some time together," Marina continued. "Alone. Like, just the two of us."

Sonny stared at her.

"We should get to know each other more," Marina said. "I would like that."

His eyes got really, really wide.

His cheeks got really, really pink.

"Um . . . I mean, I don't . . . I don't really like you . . . like that? I mean, I like you. But just as friends. I mean, we can definitely hang out if you want! But . . ."

Marina, eyes equally as wide as she realized what he thought she was saying, wanted to dig a hole and bury herself into it. "Oh my god, Sonny—that is not what I meant! Please stop talking!"

"It's not? Thank god! I mean, you're great. But I just don't like you that way!"

"Stop talking, Sonny!"

"I'm sorry!"

"I'm going inside. And if you ever tell anyone about this, I will destroy you!"

"I won't. I promise!"

Marina turned around and shut the door hard behind her. Her face felt like it was on fire. Harbor and Sam, who were finally slipping their flip-flops on to go outside, looked up at her with creased foreheads. "What's your deal?" Harbor asked.

"Nothing! Absolutely nothing!" said Marina, and she quickly sped off to disappear into her bedroom and hide there until she was absolutely certain Sonny was far, far away.

Well, so much for a sort of older brother being her safety net.

Marina didn't think she'd be going within a one-hundred-foot radius of Sonny Badger for a really, really long time.

CHAPTER TWELVE

The Ali-O'Connors' back deck was covered in strands and strands of Christmas lights. Some were still tangled up in bins. When Mama had pulled them out of the attic, she'd gotten mad at Mom. Mom was supposed to untangle them after Christmas before putting them away. She clearly hadn't.

Good Boy was going from pile to pile, sniffing everything. Mom was testing the lights to make sure they still worked, plugging each untangled strand into the electrical outlet on the dock. She'd found two already that wouldn't light up. That was okay, though. Mom, Harbor, and Sam had gone to Home Depot earlier in the week to buy more. They'd also bought sparklers—mostly because Cordelia really, really wanted them.

Sam and Harbor were crouched next to Mama, helping to inspect the lights. Harbor had already decided she didn't want any of the plain white ones. Those were Mama's favorite during the holidays. She said they made the house look nice and classy. Mom argued that the point of Christmas lights wasn't to be classy, so they also had a lot of rainbow strands. Harbor really wanted to string the boat up with those.

Harbor had banished Sonny (and Pork) from the Ali-O'Connors' house that afternoon. Even though Harbor didn't like to spend a single second away from Sonny this close to the end of summer, she also had a competitive side. It was why her school basketball team let her play with the older girls, and it was why she wouldn't let Sonny anywhere near their lights now. The Badger brothers would be decorating their grand-pa's boat. And Harbor wanted to win the prize for the best decorated boat.

Not that it mattered. Mr. Martin won every single year. He had come outside while they were untangling lights, and Mom had immediately told him to go back inside. "No cheating!" she'd yelled. Mr. Martin had cackled before doing as he was told.

Meanwhile, Cordelia was taking the strands that didn't work, pulling the lightbulbs off, and sticking them in her pockets.

"Can we have some of the extra lights to decorate Frankencrab with?" Cordelia asked.

"Fire hazard!" said Marina.

"What if we glue these sparkly ones that don't work all over Frankencrab?" Lir said. "He won't be lit up, but he might be pretty in the sun."

"Hey, now," Mom said from her crisscross-applesauce position on the dock. "Don't get distracted. We're on a mission today to get the boat ready for the weekend!"

Sam was in the middle of trying to untangle a particularly awful knot. Marina held a hand out. "I can help, if you want."

Sam shook her head. "I've got it."

"But I don't mind helping."

"I can do it, Marina," Sam said.

Marina sighed. She hadn't done it on purpose, but still she felt bad about kicking Sam. She had been trying to do nice things for her all day to make up for it.

Mom waved Marina over, a big smile on her face. "If you want to help, little fish, I would love your assistance."

Marina walked to Mom, who pulled her down into her lap. She picked up a huge stack of tangled lights and plopped them right on top of Marina. She laughed as Mom pretended to tangle Marina's hands up in the loose ends. "I can't help if I can't move," Marina said, and Mom took pity on her. She untied her, and they began to undo the mess. The whole family worked together under the bright sun, and soon the piles that were untangled were bigger than the piles that weren't.

Lir was the first to spot the swans. "Look! They're headed this way!"

There were two big swans who had lived at Sunrise Lagoon for as long as most of the Ali-O'Connor kids could remember.

They were both white, and one of them had a wing that looked a little crooked. Every year, those two swans had babies, little gray cygnets who would follow their parents in neat lines. Those small gray babies would become large gray babies, and then at the end of the summer, their feathers would turn white, just like the rest. Seven white swans made their way up the lagoon now.

"Seven swans a-swimming!" shouted Cordelia.

"Appropriate because of all the Christmas lights," Harbor muttered.

"Oh! Let's play Christmas music while we work," Marina said. She was already bopping from side to side.

"I want to feed them!" Cordelia said. But instead of being scared swans away by the volume of her voice, the swans seemed to be drawn closer. They were actually swimming faster, which Marina assumed was because they were hoping for some food. Cordelia took off running toward the house, her feet getting too close to the piles of lights for Marina's liking.

She was about to yell at her little sister, but Mom beat her to it. "Cordelia! Stop right there. No running. You know better, right? You know the rules."

Cordelia hung her head. "Yes, Mom."

"And I have those rules—all of my rules—for a reason, correct?"

"To keep us safe."

"To keep you safe," Mom agreed. "It's dangerous to run on the deck on a normal day, but we have a bunch of lights around us right now. If you trip and hit something and then land in the water, you might be too hurt to swim. This goes for everyone, even the best swimmers. So if you want to feed the swans, you will carefully walk around the lights and go inside and politely ask Mama for some bread. Okay?"

Cordelia nodded her head. "Okay."

"Thank you."

Cordelia carefully walked to the house. Extra-carefully, even, taking one slow step at a time. It took her much longer than necessary to get inside.

Marina leaned back into Mom. Her arms were solid around Marina as she worked on a giant knot. Marina's stomach had started hurting immediately when Mom asked Cordelia to stop running. She realized that Mom had taught them a lot of important rules to keep them safe on the water and in the boats. She realized that maybe she was going about this all wrong.

Mom knew how best to keep everyone safe. Mom got stuck on a boat in a really bad storm and made it back okay.

Mom was the ultimate safety net.

Marina needed to become Mom's favorite, and fast.

Boom was quick to agree with Marina's new plan. "Good! I'm glad you did some brainstorming. Let me get my camera. I want us to get this on video." Boom held her phone up at Marina. "So, Marina. How are you going to become your mom's favorite? What does your mom like best?"

Marina sighed. This was the next problem. Mom loved Mama, and boats, and fishing, and, well, boats. She also loved chartering the *Sunrise Princess*.

Marina did not like those things. And, to make matters worse, Sam and Harbor did. Mom had been teaching them all about boats, including how to fix them, for years. They already knew so much more than Marina did. There was no way she would be able to catch up.

She explained all of this to Boom, on camera.

"Well, what if we make it so that you for sure know how to fix something with the boats, like, before Sam and Harbor could? Before even your mom might be able to figure it out, too," Boom suggested.

"That's impossible."

"So, a pseudo-documentary is a documentary where the filmmakers use scripted or fake stuff to make a documentary seem real. Or sometimes real documentaries have parts of them that were staged, so that they'd be sure something they needed to happen would happen," Boom explained. "*I* take my craft seriously, but we could maybe do something small, just to help. So, basically, we'd do something to one of your mom's boats. Something small. And then when she realizes it needs to be fixed, you can suggest how to fix it. And we'd know how, since we broke it in the first place."

Marina was shaking her head throughout Boom's entire speech. "We cannot break one of my mom's boats. She would kill me. She loves those boats!"

"Not break it! Just . . . unplug the motor or something. Can you do that? Something small and fixable," Boom said.

"I don't know about this."

"Trust me," Boom said. "I won't even get the breaking part on the documentary, so that you look really smart for the final cut. Sound good?"

It sounded fishy to Marina, but she was desperate. The Parade of Lights was only a few days away. And Mom really was her best shot for feeling safe.

Before she could change her mind, Marina took Boom outside on the dock, where they stood in front of Mom's three boats. The *Sunrise Princess* was the biggest and most beautiful of the three. It was also the one that Mom needed for her business. *Raggedy Ann* was falling apart to begin with. Marina wouldn't even know where to start with that one.

Which left *Harbor Me*, the middle boat, the one they used most often as a family. Marina pointed at it. "This one, probably."

Harbor Me was in the early stages of preparation for the parade. The untangled, working strands of lights were waiting for the family to start stringing them up.

"I've never been on a boat before," Boom said. "How do we get on?"

The Ali-O'Connor kids weren't allowed on the boats without permission. Mom didn't want them playing on them. That was one of her rules. Boats weren't toys.

Marina pointed at the rope that tied *Harbor Me* to the dock. "If you tug on that, the boat will come closer. You can jump onto it from there."

Boom handed her phone to Marina. "Can you film me jumping on?"

"I guess," Marina said. "Here, let me pull the boat closer."

Marina held the rope and Boom's phone at the same time. Boom took a deep breath, then leapt onto the boat and landed safely.

Marina hesitated because there was no one on the dock to hold the rope for her.

"What if I hold on to this piling?" Boom said. "You can jump on before I let go."

Marina turned to look back at the house. They didn't have a lot of time. Someone was always going in or out. Someone was always looking through the windows. She jumped as quickly as possible. The boat bobbed up and down a bit before settling.

"Okay. Here we are!" exclaimed Boom.

Marina shushed her. "We gotta be quiet and quick. Let's find something to unplug or whatever."

The boat was over a decade old but still really nice. Everything was electronic. Marina and Boom couldn't find anything simple to mess with. They considered just pushing a bunch of buttons, but Marina nixed that idea. Even though the boat wasn't turned on and the keys were safe inside with Mom, she didn't want to risk making it move.

Boom headed toward the back, by the motor. "What's that?" she asked, pointing at a tank.

"The gas, I think."

"Oh! Once, my mom and I were driving and the car made a really funny noise, and then it jerked and stopped. My dad got real mad because my mom ran out of gas," Boom said. "What if we make it so that when your mom turns the boat on, it doesn't drive, because there's no gas."

"We can't just empty the gas, though," Marina said.

"We can find how it connects to the motor, maybe, and unplug that. So the motor doesn't get any of the gas?" Boom felt around the gas tank. There were wires where it was connected to the motor. Boom stepped aside, held her phone up, and gestured to Marina. "Go ahead, do the honors."

"I thought you weren't going to film this part," Marina said.

"I said I won't put it in the final cut," Boom clarified. "I need to film everything."

Marina sighed.

"Ready? On the count of three. One . . . two . . . three."

"Hey! Marina! What on earth do you think you're doing?" Mom's voice rang out, at the exact moment Marina reached for the wires and tugged. They came undone, but gas started splattering out, going everywhere. It got all over the boat, and into the water, making oily puddles on top of the lagoon, and all over Boom and Marina, too.

Marina knew that gas on boats sometimes caused fires, and they were also currently surrounded by electric Christmas light strands, so she immediately began screaming.

Which made Boom start screaming, too.

"What are you two doing? Are you insane?" yelled Mom, and suddenly her arms were around Marina's middle, yanking her right off the boat in one fell swoop. She pulled off Boom as well and told both of them to "Stay still! Do not move a single muscle!" Then she jumped onto the boat and got gas all over herself as she plugged everything back where it belonged.

Immediate chaos over, she hopped back onto the dock and stood in front of Boom and Marina. She wiped her hair out of her face, leaving a gas smear across her forehead. "What on earth were you thinking?" she yelled. "You are *not allowed* on the boats without me. What you just did was incredibly dangerous! What could have possibly possessed you to mess around with the motor of my boat?"

Marina hadn't gotten in this much trouble in a really, really long time.

"What's going on out here?" Mama said, swinging open the porch door and coming outside.

Marina started crying.

"You two both go stand over there so Mama can hose you down, and then I'm calling Boom's mom to come get her."

They were both damp, water dripping from their hair, as they sat on the front porch, wrapped in towels and waiting as Mama called Boom's mom. Mama had sprayed them down, as well as Mom, and now Mom was in the process of cleaning the boat. Marina was under strict orders to get into the shower as soon as Boom left, and wash off any of the gas that the hose had missed. After that, she would have to sit down with her moms. She would probably be punished. She would definitely be getting a lecture.

Marina couldn't stop crying. Mom was mad at her. Harbor still hadn't stopped blaming her for ruining her basketball hoop. She was pretty sure they had hurt Sam's feelings when they'd made her jump into the bay. Not only was Marina not any of their favorites, but she was even farther down their lists than when she had started.

"At least we're only halfway through your family," Boom said. "We still have the twins, and your mama. And we still have a few days until the parade. I was hoping we'd make progress a lot sooner, because I think it would be best to test it out somehow. Put you in fake danger so we can see who would come save you."

"Leave me alone, Boom," Marina said. "Stop talking."

Boom didn't stop talking. "Though I have to say, your mom did act as a pretty quick safety net just now. She swooped right in to fix our mess."

"Boom, stop."

"Hey! By the way, since my family doesn't have a boat yet, do you think your moms will let me come with you for the parade? It sounds so cool, and I want to ride on a boat so bad."

"I said stop, Boom!" yelled Marina. "Everyone's mad at me. You've made everything worse. I can't go to the Parade of Lights, because I *still* don't have a safety net, and it's all your fault! I never should have listened to you to begin with, so, *no*, you can't come on the boat!"

Boom grew very still. She looked away from Marina, and down at her phone in her hands. "Oh," she said quietly. "I'm sorry."

Marina didn't respond.

They sat in silence until Boom's mom came to get her.

CHAPTER THIRTEEN

It was Tuesday. The Parade of Lights was on Saturday. Harbor and Sam had spent the entire night before helping Mom wrap the lights around the boat. They had made waves along the side with the blue lights. They'd attached a Pride flag on the back, which they wrapped up in the rainbow lights. And they'd hung twinkling blue lights off the very tippy top of the boat, which spiraled down like a waterfall.

It was beautiful. It was their best work yet.

It made Marina's stomach hurt.

Mama had a bunch of glow necklaces for everyone, and Mom wrapped one around a top hat for Lir. They were going to make cookies after the parade, using M&M's and icing, to look like strings of lights.

Marina had been hoping she would be grounded and unable to join in the parade, but, of course, she had no such luck. She was only grounded from swimming in the lagoon and hanging out with Boom, two things she wasn't very interested in right now anyway.

She was currently in search of her moms to ask if she was allowed to go hang out on the deck, or if she was to be a prisoner inside the house all day. She had to go outside to ask them, which was a risk, but it seemed worth it.

They were sitting together on the chaise lounge, Mom's arms wrapped around Mama as they watched the water. It was a rare moment when they could enjoy the backyard without having to watch or fuss over any of the kids. Harbor and Sam were somewhere with Sonny, and Cordelia and Lir were up to god-knows-what in their bedroom. Good Boy was lying by their feet. He lifted his head and licked Mama's foot. She squealed and tucked her leg away.

They were watching the loons. Like ducks but with longer necks, the loons dove deep into the water to catch fish. One of Mama's favorite things was to watch them disappear into the lagoon and try and guess where they would pop out again. Sometimes it was way farther away than she'd thought. The loons could hold their breath for a while.

Mama pointed to where the loon had finally come back up for air. "There!"

"I can't believe the summer is almost over," Mom whined.

"Shh," Mama said, covering Mom's mouth with her hand until Mom swatted it away. "Don't talk about it! I'm not ready to start work again." Because Mama was a teacher, she had the summers off, which was great at Sunrise Lagoon, but she'd be starting school with Marina and her siblings come next week.

"Should we get up? I don't want to have to get up. But we have like a million things to do today." Mom sounded just like Harbor when she whined. She scratched Good Boy behind the ears.

"We'll divide and conquer," Mama said.

"Yeah, yeah. Okay. We'll ask the Badgers to keep an eye on Sam and Harbor. You take Marina to get Good Boy's nails cut. I'll take the twins to the grocery store."

"*Nooooooooooooo!*" wailed Marina. She hated running errands.

Both her moms jumped, not realizing she was right behind them. "Holy cow, how long have you been there?" Mom asked. She had her arms wrapped tightly around Mama, ready to protect her if Marina had been some kind of burglar or monster. Marina stared at Mom's arms. At least Mama always knew for sure that *she* had a safety net.

"You certainly are in no position to complain about anything right now, Miss Marina," Mom said. "Go get ready. We'll be there in a minute."

Marina sulked inside, looking for her flip-flops. She couldn't find them in the basket at the front door where they were supposed to be. She couldn't find them in her bedroom, either. Sam's were in the corner of the room, though, so Marina grabbed those. Sam sometimes got weird about sharing her things, but she didn't need to know that Marina was borrowing them. They were a little big on her, but they were flip-flops, so as long as Marina walked carefully it wouldn't matter.

Mom stuck her head through the open doorway. "Hey, Marina. You're with me. We have to pick some things up for the barbecue this weekend. You ready?"

Marina cocked her head. "I thought I was going with Mama and Good Boy."

"Mama thought we should swap," Mom said. "Which works for me. The last thing I want to have to worry about is your sister wandering."

Marina's stomach squeezed. Mama wanted to swap. Mama wanted to spend time with the twins, instead of Marina.

"Hey, you okay?" Mom asked.

"I'm fine," Marina said. "Let's just get this over with."

The grocery store was in town. Sometimes it felt like Sunrise Lagoon was in a different world than the shopping center. It was less than a ten-minute drive to get there, but the more inland they went, the more changes there were. The cool breeze they always had by the water was completely gone. It was hot and sticky by the grocery store, with humid and thick summer air. It also seemed darker without the water to reflect the sun. Even the seagulls that swooped around the parking lot looking for crumbs and garbage seemed different, like the farther they got from the water, the grayer their feathers became.

Mom parked the car and handed Marina a quarter. "Go get us a shopping cart."

Marina hurried over to the row of shopping carts stacked together. She had to put the quarter in the slot of the cart at the end and tug to get it loose. Mom always complained that it was an outdated practice. None of the other grocery stores in the area required them to have a quarter just to get a shopping cart. Marina pressed the quarter in and had to pull at the cart a couple times before it wiggled free.

She pushed the cart over to Mom, who placed a hand at Marina's back, and they made their way into the grocery store.

Mama had handwritten a shopping list for Mom, which also seemed outdated, in Marina's opinion. Mom unfolded it, and Marina scowled at the length. "I thought you said we only needed to pick up *some* things."

"This *is* only some things. You should see the regular weekly list if you think this one is long." Mom laughed.

They got to work. Mom grabbed a frozen bag of shrimp, a ton of chicken, and some Sweet Baby Ray's barbecue sauce. Over at produce, Marina helped pick out the best-looking ears of corn. They pulled back the corn husks to make sure the insides were perfect. (Marina almost gagged when she found black, wrinkled kernels on one of them.) Mom picked out some big tomatoes so Mama could make tabbouleh, and some cucumbers, too. She sent Marina to choose a watermelon, but Marina didn't trust herself to pick it up without dropping it.

They were headed toward the bakery when Marina accidentally flipped Sam's flip-flop right off her foot. "Whoops," she said, and hopped on one foot over to it.

"Having shoe trouble?" Mom said.

"These aren't mine," Marina admitted. "And I guess Sam has very big feet."

"Hang on to the cart," Mom said. "I'll push you."

Marina hesitated. She hadn't clung on to the shopping cart while one of her moms pushed in a really long time. Usually it was Cordelia and Lir who hung all over it like monkeys.

Mom tapped on the cart. "Come on."

Marina stepped up on the bottom rack and held on to the front of the cart. "Okay. But be careful," she said.

"Like this, you mean?" Mom said, and then shoved on the cart superhard without letting go.

Marina squealed and held on tighter as she jerked forward. It sent tingles all through her body, her heart pounding, but it also made her laugh.

"Mom!" she exclaimed.

"You act like I'd ever let something happen to you," Mom said, pushing the cart gently now, and at a normal speed. She threw some bread into the shopping cart and then wheeled it toward the deli. "I would never."

Marina thought really carefully about that.

"Ham or turkey for the week?" Mom asked.

"Um." Marina paused. Harbor and Cordelia liked ham best, but both Sam and Lir liked turkey more. She liked both, so she never really had much of a say in the weekly debate. If she got to choose, though . . . "Turkey, I guess. But . . . can we maybe get salami, too?"

"You've got it," Mom said. She pulled a number tab at the deli counter so they could wait their turn to order.

Marina watched Mom as she tucked a strand of straight blond hair behind her ear and looked down at the list in her hand. She was crossing off the things they'd already found. Marina had her hair in the usual giant bun on top of her head. She reached to tuck the loose pieces behind her ears, like Mom. Hers wouldn't stay in place. "Mom?" Marina said.

"Hmm?" Mom said, still looking at her list.

"Do you know who your favorite is? Of all of us, I mean."

Mom jerked her head up to look at Marina. "Like, of you kids, you mean?"

"Yes," Marina said. "Everybody has a favorite everything."

"Not me," Mom said.

"That's not true."

"It is! I love you all exactly the same."

"That's impossible," Marina said. "Is it Harbor? Because you had her first? Because you actually were pregnant with her?"

"Nope," Mom said.

"Sam, then? Because you both love boats more than anyone should love boats?"

Mom softly laughed. "Marina, no. I don't have a favorite. I promise."

Marina ran her fingers along the shopping cart. "I don't go on the boats with you anymore. So I know it's not me."

"Hey," Mom said, her voice sharp. She walked over to Marina, tugging her off the shopping cart and kneeling in front of her. She looked Marina directly in the eyes, hands gripping her arms gently. "I love all of you. I don't have a favorite. But even if I did, do you really think you'd not be in the running? Marina, I adore you."

Marina shrugged.

"I'll tell you what," Mom said. "I have a favorite thing about each of you. Do you want to hear that list? I love that Harbor is stubborn. I don't necessarily love it when that stubbornness is directed at me, but she's such a strong kid. She'll be a force to reckon with as she gets older. And I love how gentle Sam is. She approaches everything with such thoughtfulness. I don't think I could ever be as kind and considerate as she is. I love how excited Cordelia is to learn and explore and experiment. Even if that excitement leads to crab monsters on my back deck. I love how Lir is always one hundred percent Lir, no matter what. Lir doesn't care what other people think—Lir is just Lir. Which is something I wasn't ever able to do until I was much, much older."

The deli worker behind called out, "Nine," which was Mom's number. Marina expected her to take her turn. She didn't. "What I love most about you, Marina, is that you're always asking these big questions. You worry *so much*, and that worries *me*, but you're constantly trying to find solutions, and you're always making sure that everyone is safe. You've got a big heart, little fish."

Marina blushed. "They called your number," she said.

"Listen to me. Every single one of you brings something special to this family. And I love *that* the most. I love that each and every piece of this puzzle that your mama and I worked so hard to create has come together perfectly," Mom said. She placed a warm hand against Marina's cheek. "Does that make sense? Do you understand?"

"I guess so," Marina said.

"And also I love your ridiculous dance moves. I'm pretty sure you get those from me." Mom kissed Marina on the top of her head. "I'm going to grab this turkey and salami, and then you and I are going to pick out a piece of candy each, if you promise not to tell anyone—including Mama."

They finished up quickly after that. Mom picked out a KitKat, her favorite, while Marina grabbed a Reese's. They gobbled them up before they even got back to the car. Marina helped Mom unload and then clung on to the shopping cart as Mom went to put it away. She picked up speed, zigzagging and spinning the cart until Marina couldn't stop laughing.

"Oh, shoot," Mom said as they climbed into the car. "I forgot to take the quarter back."

Marina laughed even harder.

They drove toward Sunrise Lagoon, where the sun beamed brighter, reflecting off the water, and the breeze picked up, and even the seagulls seemed lighter as they flew over the car and into the marshlands. Mom smiled at Marina through the rearview mirror and Marina thought, *Maybe running errands with Mom isn't so bad after all.*

Mama, Cordelia, and Lir got home first. Good Boy was sporting a brand-new bandanna, a green one that said he was a GOOD BOY. The twins were rolling around on the floor with him. Good Boy did that anytime he got shampooed—he'd roll around until he didn't feel damp anymore, even if the groomers had blow-dried him.

Marina kicked Sam's flip-flops off, leaving them by the front door. Mama came over and wrapped her arms around her. "Successful trip?"

Marina shoved away from Mama, wiggling out of her grasp. "It was fine," she snapped.

"Hey, Marina, what's with the attitude?" Mom chimed in, sounding confused.

"I'm going to my room."

Marina took off before either of her moms could call her

back. She flopped onto her bed, burying her face in her pillow. She didn't look up when there was a knock on her door. When the knock was paired with a not-so-subtle cough, Marina did pick her head up. Harbor was standing in the doorway. "What?" Marina asked.

"You hurt Mama's feelings, you know."

She hurt mine first! Marina thought, but she didn't respond out loud.

"Hey, so . . ." Harbor began.

"Shouldn't you be busy hanging with Sonny?"

"Sonny's grandparents are making them do a family dinner, since they leave on Monday. I don't want to talk about it." Harbor walked over to the side of Marina's bed and pulled her pillow out from under her. Marina sat up and glared at her. "Anyway. *So . . .*" Harbor repeated, pointedly, "there's actually a WNBA game on TV today. Which, you know, doesn't happen a lot, because no one takes girls' sports seriously. Which isn't fair at all, and they need to seriously stop perpetuating old ideas and, like, get with the times."

"Ugh, you sound like Mama. You're just repeating what she says."

"It's true, though!" Harbor said. "Anyway the game is on, in like ten minutes."

"Okay?"

"Do you want to watch with me?"

Marina glanced at her warily. "What?"

"You don't have to," Harbor added quickly. "It's just, you seemed to want to watch the other day. You asked, like, a million questions that would be kind of annoying if you didn't actually care about the answers. So . . . you cared, right? And you wanted to play the other day and everything. So do you want to watch—yes or no? It starts soon, and I don't want to miss tip-off."

Marina was stunned. She wished Boom was here to get this on camera. Though given how much trouble Boom kept causing, it was probably for the best her phone wasn't in Marina's face anymore.

Still, though. She'd had a decent trip with Mom, even though Mom had been so mad at her and Boom for messing with the boat. Maybe Marina could turn things around with Harbor, too. "Yeah," she said. "Okay. I'll watch with you."

Mama was in the kitchen making dinner, the twins were outside with Good Boy, and Sam was on the boat with Mom to go up the lagoon and down the river for more gas, since the boat was now low on it. Which meant it was just Harbor and Marina, alone, sitting on the couch, watching the basketball game.

Marina recognized one of the players from her nightmares. "Hey! That's Diana Taurasi!"

Harbor smiled really big. "Yeah, it is. Good job!"

Marina watched Diana Taurasi run up and down the court, making three-point shots like wild, while Harbor told Marina more about her favorite players and her favorite teams, and said, "Maybe you'll understand more now when you come to watch me play," and "You were so close. When Mom *finally* gets me a new basketball hoop, we should try and make those bounce shots again."

When Mama announced that dinner was ready, Harbor asked if they could wait until halftime. They ate fast, and kept watching, and Diana Taurasi's team won, and Marina realized she couldn't wait to tell Boom that maybe something had actually worked, after all.

CHAPTER FOURTEEN

Most years, the weather stayed hot and humid in New Jersey through September. It still felt like summer, even into the early fall. Still, there were telltale signs that summer was ending. The ospreys that made their nests atop the high wooden plank built in the marshes in the sanctuary for that purpose, that laid their eggs in the early spring, were now gone. The eggs had hatched, the babies had grown, and they'd all flown away. The baby swans had grown and would soon leave, too.

The sun set earlier now. On the Fourth of July, the Ali-O'Connors had to wait until much later for the sky to grow dark to watch the fireworks. Night would come almost an hour earlier for Labor Day. The stores had put out their back-to-school supplies, and Mama had begun taking advantage of those sales. Sam and Marina already had new backpacks. Harbor had new basketball shoes. Lir and Cordelia, who had both gone through growth spurts, received whole new wardrobes.

Even the beaches weren't as crowded anymore. There were fewer boats on the water. Vacations had been used up, and schools in some neighboring towns had already started. The Badger brothers were packing to go home.

The Ali-O'Connor kids took note of these things as they happened. Summer on Sunrise Lagoon was the most special time of all. Soon, just like every year, it would come to an end.

Marina had gone almost the entire summer without going on her family's boats. That, too, would come to an end soon. She stood on the deck, looking at them. The boats wouldn't be there much longer, either. Mom would drive them, one at a time, to the boat launch at the end of the lagoon. She would hook them up to the trailer on her car, and she would pull them out of the water and drive them to Joe Koch's marina, where they would be safely wrapped and stored for winter. The lagoon would look bare without them.

Marina found herself thinking, *I don't want it to end.*

Across the lagoon, where the Patels' dog used to bark its little head off, the screen door opened and Boom and her mother came outside. They were watering the plants and flowers Boom's mom had decorated the backyard with. Marina lifted her hand in a small wave, but Boom turned and look away.

Well, fine. Be that way. If anyone had a right to be angry, it was Marina.

And she *was* angry. And maybe a little scared. The Parade of Lights was so soon. *Harbor Me* was all ready to go. Marina had promised she would be on it. She wanted to take back that promise.

She couldn't do this. She couldn't go on that boat. Because there were over two thousand boat accidents a year. And because no matter what Mom said, everyone had favorites. No one would reach for Marina.

"Hey."

Marina jumped at the sound of Mama's voice. "Oh. Hi."

Mama didn't wrap an arm around her this time. "What're you doing?"

"Just looking."

"At the boat?"

Marina shrugged.

"It looks really pretty. You all did such a wonderful job decorating it," Mama said.

"I didn't decorate it. Harbor and Sam did."

"Mom said you helped with the lights, though."

"I guess."

Mama didn't respond. They stood side by side, looking out at the lagoon. Marina noticed their shadows stretching out in front of them. They started out as two separate figures—Marina and Mama—but as they continued and grew, they became one.

"Do you want to talk about Saturday?" Mama asked.

"No," Marina answered quickly. "What about it?"

"Mom said you promised you were going on the boat for the parade," Mama said. "Is that still the plan?"

Marina looked again at *Harbor Me*. She didn't want to keep her promise, but what was the alternative? If she broke her promise, Mom would be disappointed. If she broke her promise, her moms would ask why. They would keep asking. She had gone all summer making excuses, and keeping away from the boats, and knowing exactly what to say so that everyone would leave her alone. She couldn't keep doing that.

Part of her wanted to ask Mama the same thing she asked Mom in the grocery store: *Do you know who your favorite is?* She wanted Mama to tell her all the things she loved about everyone, just like Mom had done.

But Mama *did* have a favorite. Even though she and Mom had adopted Marina, Marina wasn't enough for Mama. Mama wanted to have her *own* babies. Mama wanted to have the twins. Marina couldn't compete with that. They had been Mama's favorite ever since. They were the ones Mama wanted to run errands with, not Marina.

Marina's chest felt tight.

Something clanged loudly right behind them. They both jumped, turning to see what the noise was. Another part of Frankencrab had come tumbling to the deck. It attracted a couple of seagulls, who swooped down low enough that both Marina and Mama had to duck out of the way.

"That stupid thing is going to get us pooped on," Marina grumbled.

Mama laughed. "Mom's not too thrilled with it falling apart all over her deck, either. I can't let her get rid of it yet, though. Cordelia and Lir worked so hard on it, and they love it so much. I want them to be able to enjoy it as much as possible."

Marina tried not to roll her eyes. Of course Mama wanted Cordelia and Lir to have exactly what they wanted, regardless of the fact that everyone else absolutely did not.

"You know, I never got a chance to really talk to you about that day at the beach," Mama said. Marina felt her whole body get stiff, but before she could say anything, Mama continued. "I don't think I ever told any of you this, but I used to get panic attacks."

Marina carefully glanced at her out of the side of her eye. "What do you mean?"

"They started when I was in high school. I think I was starting to figure out that I liked girls the way I thought I was supposed to like boys. I went to a really, really small school. If anyone had found out, well . . . I don't think they'd have been nice to me," Mama said. "And my parents—your grandparents—they eventually understood, but I was really afraid about telling them. And keeping those feelings to myself, it was too much sometimes. I was so scared. And then I'd be in a situation that made me nervous, and my chest would get really tight and I'd have a really hard time breathing. It was awful. But you know that, don't you?"

Marina shrugged. "It's fine. I was just scared, at the beach, because of Cordelia."

"I think it might be more than that. And I just wanted you to know, I understand. I really do. And if you ever want to talk to someone about it, you can talk to me," Mama said. "And . . . And I think we're going to make an appointment for you to talk to a counselor, like Sam does. Like we talked about."

"What? No!" shouted Marina. This was all a trap. She knew it! "I told you I was fine. It was just because Cordelia wandered off like she always does and I was worried she drowned! And . . . And I'm going on the stupid boat this weekend!"

"There's nothing wrong with talking to someone, just so that—"

"It's because I'm adopted, isn't it?" Marina said.

Mama's eyes opened wide. "What? Wait, Marina. You're taking this the wrong way. Maybe I'm not saying it right."

"Sam sees a counselor because she was adopted, and you want me to see one because I'm different, too. Maybe you should have just had the twins first, and not me at all!"

Mama took a deep breath and reached out to grasp Marina's shoulder. "Okay. I think we need to—"

"Don't touch me," Marina said, ducking out of the way. "I don't want to talk about *this* anymore. I don't want to talk to *you* anymore."

"Something is wrong, Marina. Something you're not telling me," Mama said. "Why won't you talk to me anymore? You're pushing me away, and I'm just trying to understand *why*."

Mama's eyes got wet, and it made Marina's stomach hurt even more. Marina's eyes started to burn with tears, too. "Please can I just go inside? Please can we just stop talking now?"

Mama took a deep, wobbly breath. "Okay. Okay, go ahead."

Marina hesitated. Mama seemed smaller than Marina thought she was. Maybe Marina was just taller now. Maybe she, like the twins, had had her own growth spurt this summer. Maybe one day she would grow taller than Mama, and taller than Mom, and taller than all of them. She didn't know how tall her birth parents were. It was possible they were giants. It was possible that, someday, Marina would find a magic bean, and a beanstalk would grow, and she would climb up and find them.

The thought startled Marina. She hadn't realized she even *wanted* to maybe find her birth parents until just now.

Which made her chest grow even tighter, which made her eyes even wetter. Because she loved being an Ali-O'Connor. She didn't want to be part of some other family.

What, then, *did* she want?

Mama sighed. "Come on, Marina." She held out a hand. Marina looked at it for a moment.

But then she took it, and Mama led them both inside.

CHAPTER FIFTEEN

Before the Ali-O'Connors started fostering Sam, their moms sat everyone in the living room. Harbor was eight, Marina was only six. The twins, at three, weren't so good at sitting still on the couch, usually wriggling up and down and bouncing from one side to the other. Not that they were good at sitting still now, either. But their moms had explained that it was important for everyone, including the twins, to put on their very best listening ears.

The seriousness of the moment seemed to make Harbor anxious, and it even made the twins stop squirming. Marina, though she was only two the last time they'd had a conversation like this, remembered it quite clearly and knew what was coming. Her guess was confirmed when Mom said, "How would you little fish feel about Mama and me making this family bigger?"

Harbor glanced down the couch at the rest of her siblings. "Bigger?"

Marina understood exactly how she felt. She was still getting used to the last two additions to the Ali-O'Connor family. When Cordelia and Lir were babies, they would cry and cry, and Mama would rush to hold them, and Marina would imagine putting them up for adoption. Now that she was older, she knew that wasn't how adoption worked. Moms didn't get rid of their babies just because they were annoying. They decided to put their babies up for adoption because they couldn't take care of them, and Marina's moms could take care of their family just fine. This was a relief, because Marina felt safe here. It was also awful, because they were having a conversation about having even more babies to bring into the Ali-O'Connor fold.

She sank into the couch, wondering if Mama would carry the new baby in her stomach again and if they would end up with twins again, and thinking how absolutely terrible two more Cordelias and Lirs would be.

It was Mom who said, "We wanted to know your thoughts about us adopting another child again."

And that changed everything. It was exciting for Marina! She wouldn't be the only one who was adopted anymore. Plus, if they adopted another baby, just like they did with her, then that would make her officially one of the older siblings, with Cordelia and Lir in the middle. Harbor wouldn't be the only boss of everyone anymore. *Marina* could be the boss of everyone, too. Marina could also be the best big sister to the new adopted baby, because no one else would know what it was like to be adopted, and everyone would stop fussing over the twins and start focusing on the new baby, too.

All of Marina's plans went right out of the window when their moms didn't bring home a baby, and instead brought home eight-year-old Sam.

Now, though, Sam was the one who would understand more than anyone else how Marina might be feeling. She had a birth mom she didn't really remember, the same way Marina didn't know her anything about hers. But Sam, unlike Marina, had a birth grandmother she used to live with. Sam had an entire life before she came to live with the Ali-O'Connors. Maybe she sometimes thought about that life—and her birth mom and birth dad. Maybe she sometimes thought about what would have happened if her grandma hadn't gotten too sick to take care of her. Maybe she sometimes thought about a house above a beanstalk, with giants, who were really her parents, waiting up there for her to come home.

Marina's stomach felt all twisted up and awful, her chest tight. She didn't really believe in giants. But she couldn't stop thinking about them reaching down and scooping her up and taking her away from here. Her giant mom would be Mexican, too. And maybe she would sing to Marina in Spanish. And maybe if she sang enough, Marina would know how to sing in Spanish, too.

Part of her wanted that to happen.

The other part of her absolutely, certainly, one hundred percent did not.

Maybe Sam would understand. Maybe Sam had a family of giants in her head, too.

It took forever to find a moment to get Sam alone. Luckily for Marina, Cordelia and Lir had gotten ridiculously salty and sandy in the bay that afternoon, and Mama was giving them a bath at the same time Mom had to deal with an epic Harbor meltdown. Harbor, who sometimes had emotions too big for her body, was leaking those emotions all over the place in anticipation of Sonny Badger going home and school starting next week.

This meant that somewhere, Sam was alone. Good Boy was occupied with ripping a leg off a Lamb Chop toy. When he saw Marina, he dropped the toy and wagged his tail at her, with his slobbery tongue dangling out of his mouth. She gave his head a pat before resuming her search. There were only so many places Sam could be in their small, crowded house.

Which meant Sam was outside.

Marina crept out the back door. The sun was still in the sky, but it was low. The sky was still blue, but pinks were creeping in from the bottom. The clouds that passed by overhead were casting more shadows than earlier in the day. Sam was standing at the edge of the dock, her toes curled over it, looking down at the lagoon in front of her.

"What're you doing?" Marina asked.

Sam jumped, startled. "Oh. Nothing."

"Doesn't look like nothing."

"Well, it is."

"Mama is helping the twins with their bath, and Mom is dealing with Hurricane Harbor, so if you're thinking about going in the lagoon, you shouldn't. Because no one is watching you," Marina said. Seeing Sam so close to the edge made her stomach clench. She still wasn't used to Sam not wearing a life vest.

Sam pointed across the street. The Badgers' grandpa was standing at their grill. He waved at Marina, who waved back. Sam explained, "I was swimming with Sonny. His mom called, so he had to go inside. But his grandpa is still watching me swim. Mama knows."

"Well, you're not swimming anyway. You're just standing here."

"I'm trying to jump in," Sam said. Then, more determinedly: "I *want* to jump in."

"Oh. Okay."

"Can you please go back inside?"

"I wanted to talk to you. It's important," Marina said, then she paused, watching Sam. "You can go ahead and jump, you know."

"I will."

"Okay."

"I'm gonna."

"Then do it."

Sam scrunched her face up and bent her legs like she was a spring. She started breathing from her nose, then took one big, deep inhale. Marina waited, watching.

But Sam didn't jump. She exhaled like a deflating balloon, and stood up straight, even though her shoulders were slumped. Her cheeks were flushed. "What do you want, Marina?"

Marina looked from Sam to the lagoon and then back again. Something clicked into place. "Oh," Marina said. "You know, I really did accidentally kick you last time we jumped. It wasn't your fault your jump went wonky."

"Fine. Okay. I'm not thinking about that anyway."

"I think you are," Marina said. "I'm pretty sure that's why you didn't actually jump just now. Am I right? I'm pretty sure I'm right."

Sam didn't respond.

"Do you want me to jump with you?" Marina wasn't sure why she asked. Part of her was hoping Sam would say no, because she didn't want to jump into the lagoon.

Sam sighed. "You don't have your bathing suit on."

"I can go put it on."

"It's almost dark out."

"Yeah, but it's not dark yet."

"You hate going in the lagoon."

Marina put her hands on her hips. "Yes, I do. So this is a one-time offer, and you should consider yourself super lucky I'm even making it." She thought for a moment. "*And* the next time I want to go to the park instead of going swimming, you should take my side against Harbor's."

Sam got really, really quiet. The smell of Jim Badger's burgers wafted across the lagoon, making Marina's stomach hurt a little more than it already was. She wanted to call over and tell him she was pretty sure he was overcooking them. She opened her mouth to do just that, but then Sam finally said, "Okay. Okay, let's jump in together."

Marina got her bathing suit on as quickly as humanly possible so she didn't change her mind. Sam probably wouldn't appreciate that, and this was pretty much all Marina and Boom's fault anyway, for making Sam jump with them in the first place. When she went back outside, Sam was standing in the exact same spot, staring at the water. The Badger family was sitting on their porch, eating the burned-smelling burgers. Sam's face was still pink, and Marina was worried that now that Sonny and George and everyone were outside watching, Sam might change her mind.

Marina came to stand right next to her. "You've jumped before," she said.

"I know," Sam answered quickly. "But just with Mom. Or with a life vest on. Or with you and Boom and Sonny, and I didn't like that. That didn't feel good."

"I'm sorry," Marina said. "You don't have to jump if you don't want to."

"I *do* want to."

Marina tried to remember everything she'd learned back when she was little and Mom had taught her to jump from this very dock. It had been so long ago she almost couldn't even picture it. They'd all just known how to jump. Except for Sam, who'd come to live with them later. "You just gotta let the gravity take you down a bit, and not fight it. And then you let the water help you rise. You just gotta kick and swim up. I'll help you, if you need."

Sam kept staring down at the water. "Can I hold your hand?"

Marina wiped it against her bathing suit first. It was a little sweaty. "Yeah."

Sam took Marina's hand. Marina inched her toes over the edge of the deck, like Sam. The water was dark and murky in the lagoon. Sometimes, Marina could see crabs along the pilings of the deck, and sometimes little fish would jump and make ripples. Mostly, though, if there was something swimming underneath the water, there was no way of knowing. "We should count to three," Marina said. "And then just do it."

"Okay," Sam said.

"You should count," Marina added.

If Marina counted down and Sam wasn't ready, Marina would jump anyway, without knowing. Since they were holding hands, she would tug Sam right in. Which was probably what had happened when Boom counted to three the other day.

Sam took a deep, deep breath. "I'm ready."

"Okay."

"One," Sam said, curling her toes over the deck. "Two . . ."

Marina closed her eyes and held her breath and bent her knees.

"Three!"

They jumped. The water was cold. Marina almost lost her grip on Sam's hand when they hit the water. She didn't, though. She held on tightly, and as she began kicking toward the surface, she was extra-careful not to kick Sam.

Marina broke the surface first, taking a big gulp of air as she tugged Sam up by the hand. Sam popped up and took a big breath, too, but this time she wasn't coughing. She blinked and wiped the water from her eyes and faced Marina with the world's biggest smile on her face. "We did it!" she said. "I told you I could!"

It wasn't until much later, at the dinner table, when Sam was telling Mom all about how she'd been working on her jumps off the deck and how she'd soon be able to do them all by herself, that Marina realized she never actually asked Sam about being adopted.

CHAPTER SIXTEEN

That night, their neighbor Jamie Perez and four of her friends were shooting fireworks over the marshlands. They had firecrackers and ground spinners, and Roman candles. The whole sky lit up. There were loud cracking sounds. Good Boy was hiding in the bathroom. Mr. Martin threatened to call the police, though Jamie knew by now he was all talk, and she and her friends kept lighting them.

Mama made a point of telling the Ali-O'Connor children that setting off fireworks was dangerous, but the entire family gathered on the back deck to watch anyway. Unlike on the Fourth of July, when the entire neighborhood was out and barbecuing and partying, when the Ali-O'Connor kids buzzed with summer energy that kept them awake far past their bedtime, tonight they watched quietly. It was Thursday night. The Parade of Lights was in two days. Two mornings after that, the

Badger brothers would go home to Staten Island. Then school would start the very next day.

The end of the summer was a weekend away, and Jamie Perez's fireworks show felt like the beginning of the goodbyes.

Cordelia sat in Mama's lap, and Lir was up on Mom's shoulders. Marina was sandwiched by Harbor and Sam. Even though the air was a little chilly and they were all wearing sweatshirts over their summer clothes, Marina was warm. She felt like Sam and Harbor actually wanted to stand there with her. Even though Marina thought she would feel nervous, because Mama said it was dangerous and Marina didn't really trust Jamie and her friends, she wasn't.

Across the lagoon, the Badger brothers came outside. Brenda Badger, their grandmother, shouted that she would also call the police if Jamie didn't knock it off. Mom repeated what Mrs. Badger said, mumbling it, using her very best Mrs. Badger voice. Mama reached up to lightly slap Mom on the shoulder to get her to stop.

Mr. Martin and Mr. Harris were watching together from Mr. Harris's back deck, even though Mr. Martin had been grumbling about it. Mr. Martin caught sight of Marina and yelled over, "Miss Marina! You coming by to play cards soon? I can beat you in poker after my boat beats your family's in the parade tomorrow!"

"You won't beat us in the parade, and you won't beat Marina, either," Mom called over. She winked at Marina, who smiled.

Boom and her mom came outside to watch, too. Marina didn't try waving. She didn't think it would matter anyway. It was dark, and with the glow of the fireworks, it'd be hard to see if Boom waved back.

Marina sighed, standing between the warmth of her sisters, because she'd made real progress with them. She wanted to tell Boom all about it: Harbor asking her to watch WNBA games, helping Sam jump off the dock. She even wanted to tell Boom about her grocery trip with Mom, how she was pretty sure Mom had forgiven them for the whole incident on the boat.

Which meant that first thing in the morning, Marina would have to bite the bullet and try to make up with Boom.

But that was tomorrow. For now, she would keep watching the fireworks with her family.

At first, Marina figured she should wait until after breakfast to knock on Boom's door. It was only polite to make sure Boom and her mom were awake and ready before she showed up. By the time Marina figured it was safe, it was pretty close to lunchtime. She didn't want to interrupt them eating, either. So, she ate all of her peanut butter sandwich slowly, including the crusts.

But she really couldn't make any more excuses. The Parade of Lights was tomorrow. Tomorrow! She tried not to think about that yet. She tried to focus on the task at hand, which was going to Boom's house to talk to Boom. Something she had done a bunch of times. Easy-peasy. She could do this. She tied her sneakers. Didn't think they were tied well enough. Undid them and tied them again. And then Marina scolded herself, because she was being ridiculous.

Boom's house was one of the only ones on the street with a giant tree in front, and as Marina walked past it, a whole bunch of birds flew out. She shrieked and then shook her head. "Good grief," she said, and knocked sharply three times on the door.

Boom answered immediately. "Oh! Marina! Hi!"

"Hi, Boom. We should talk."

"Okay, yeah. You're right. Sure." Boom held the door open wider. "Want to come inside?"

Marina kept her head held high as she walked into Boom's house and immediately headed for the stairs to go to Boom's room. Boom followed her. As Marina sat down on the bed, she was startled when she heard purring. Amato was lying on the bed behind her. He got up and stretched, like a proper Halloween-style cat, before crawling into Marina's lap.

"Okay. So please don't yell at me again," Boom said, hovering at her door. "I didn't mean to make you mad, or to get us in trouble. I'm really sorry. My mom says sometimes I'm too eager and it makes me bossy. I don't mean to be bossy. Do you think I'm bossy? Is that why you don't want to be friends?"

"I still want to be friends," Marina said.

Boom sighed with her entire body. She basically turned into Jell-O, slumping against her wall. "Oh, thank the stars. That's great! That's amazing news!"

"I'm sorry, too. That I yelled at you, I mean. Especially because I think you were maybe right this whole time."

"Right about what?" Boom asked.

Amato yawned in Marina's face. She scrunched up her nose. He had breath as bad as Good Boy's. "Our plan. The things we tried, with Harbor and Sam? They didn't work the first time we did them, but they worked later. I think they both like me again. Mom, too, actually. And, well, I'll explain it all, but I'm really sorry you didn't get it on camera."

Boom jumped up and ran over to her desk, where her phone was plugged into its charger. "That's okay! We can do dramatic reenactments. Or we can do the whole confessional thing, where you recap what happened. I can ask my dad his advice when he gets home."

"When *is* your dad getting home?"

"Not for a bit yet. It's fine. That gives me plenty of time to put together a first cut of our documentary to show him," Boom said. "I told him all about it on the phone. I mean, before we fought. So I'm excited to show him when it's done. He'll like it. I know it—don't worry. *Hey! Can I come on the boat for the Parade of Lights, then?*"

Marina had to cover her ears as Boom shouted that last bit. And she was a little overwhelmed by how quickly Boom had gotten over their fight. "Probably," she said. "Yeah. I mean, I'll have to ask my mom, but she usually says yes if there's enough room. And since the Badgers have their own boat, it should be fine."

Boom held up her phone. Marina had almost missed having the camera in her face. *Almost.* "That's good. Then I'll be there, too, when you finally go on the boat again."

Marina froze. Amato, still in her lap, did not appreciate that she'd stopped petting him. He reached a paw up to bat lightly at her chin until she resumed his head scratches. "It's tomorrow, you know. One day away. And maybe things went pretty well with Harbor and Sam and Mom, but I don't know for sure if I'm anyone's favorite. I still don't know if I'd have a safety net."

"Well, I'll be there," Boom said again. "And I told you I already thought about that. We need to run a test. Remember I said so? It was right before we fought, so maybe you don't. We need to put you in fake peril so we can see who would come save you."

"That sounds dangerous."

"Eh, fake dangerous."

"When would we do it?"

"We'd have to do it tomorrow morning, or afternoon. Before the Parade of Lights."

"*What* would we do? And before you suggest it, I'm not going up on a roof."

"Okay. That's fine. But you know what I'm going to say, don't you?" Boom had one hand on her hip and the other holding her phone tight. She sat down on the couch next to Marina, flipping the phone camera so it was on selfie mode as she squeezed her head into the frame. Her forehead tapped a little too hard against Marina's, and Amato leapt out of Marina's lap. Boom smiled at the camera. "We will have to brainstorm!"

Marina laughed and pushed Boom away. "Okay. Fine. We'll brainstorm. You'll come over tomorrow, then?"

"I will come over tomorrow, then."

"Okay. Then I should get going. I told my moms I'd only be here for a little bit," Marina said. She jumped off the bed and headed for the door.

"Hey, Marina?" Boom called after her.

"Yeah?"

Boom gave her one of those superbig entirely-all-teeth Boom smiles. "I'm really, really glad we're friends again."

Marina couldn't help but smile back. "Me too."

After dinner, Harbor, Sam, and Marina all ended up in their bedroom earlier than usual for a summer night. The Badgers were spending time with their grandparents, and Harbor was lying in bed, clenching her jaw, obviously trying to ignore the fact that tomorrow would be her last day with Sonny in a very, very long time. There were over two hundred fifty days between Labor Day and Memorial Day, when Sonny and his brothers would come back.

Sam was finishing her last summer reading book. Unlike Marina and Harbor—who hated having to do homework in the summer, and weren't even close to finishing theirs.

Marina wasn't moping like Harbor or doing schoolwork like Sam. She was just minding her own business, trying not to think about the fact that she was going to have to get on *Harbor Me* tomorrow.

Maybe. Probably. Oh, would it really be so bad if she didn't? Mom would be absolutely disappointed, and Mama would want to have more of her talks and send Marina to counseling like Sam, and she would be the only one in the family who didn't go on the boats, and she would keep getting left behind as they rode off, waving at her, and she would never be close enough to be anyone's favorite ever, and—

She could do this. She could.

The bedroom door suddenly cracked open. The oldest three Ali-O'Connor sisters picked their heads up to see who was intruding. One small, round twin head (Cordelia's) popped through the crack, followed by another small, round twin head (Lir's) a little bit lower. They hadn't knocked.

"You're supposed to knock," Harbor shouted at them.

"We aren't here to talk to *you*," Cordelia said. An arm snaked through the door, pointing directly at Marina.

"Can you please come meet us in our room, Marina?" Lir said.

"Right now?"

Cordelia and Lir nodded their heads, their wavy hair bouncing all over the place. "Yes, please. It's important!" added Cordelia.

"Shut the door behind you," Harbor said.

Marina followed Cordelia and Lir into their bedroom. She was barely over the threshold when Cordelia slammed the door shut. "What are you doing?" said Marina.

Lir was hopping back and forth from one foot to the other. "We need your help. I need your help. We made a mistake. I don't like it."

"We don't want to get in trouble, either," Cordelia said. "So we can't ask moms for help."

"Just tell me what you did," Marina said, crossing her arms over her chest as she assumed the role of big sister.

Lir tugged on her arm. "Over here."

Marina gasped when she saw it: a huge, damp, greenish something spreading all over Cordelia and Lir's rug. Cordelia immediately launched into an explanation when she saw Marina's face. "So we didn't mean to! I was trying to make slime. But not regular slime! I wanted to make slime that we could use to catch seagulls but that wouldn't hurt them—that's why Lir was helping. Lir was going to make sure that if we trapped them, we could study them but then let them go and they'd be fine and they'd be able to get all the slime off perfectly. But, well, then . . ." Cordelia gestured to the rug.

Lir was close to tears and breathing kind of funny. "Please, can you help? Can we wash the rug, like when we washed the blanket?"

Marina had no idea how to wash a rug. It wasn't like she could pick the entire thing up and chuck it into the washing machine. She wasn't even convinced a washing machine would take care of this giant green smudge. They were right about one thing, Mama would absolutely freak out if she saw it.

Lir was breathing even louder now. "Please, Marina? Please help?"

Marina groaned inwardly. "Okay. You know that spray stuff that Mama uses when Good Boy barfs up crabs and grass on the carpet? She keeps it under the sink. Go find that and bring it back to me."

Cordelia and Lir immediately took off running.

"And paper towels! Grab those, too," Marina called after them.

They were back in record time, handing Marina the spray bottle and towels. Marina went right to work, covering all the green smudges. It foamed up a bit when it hit the rug. Earlier in the summer, the lagoon water had been foamy, too. The foam had pushed its way along the edges of the dock to the dead end of the lagoon. It had looked just like this. The longer this carpet-cleaning foam sat, the greener it got, as it soaked into the failed slime.

"How long do we wait?" Cordelia asked. "I like this rug stuff. Can I spray it somewhere else?"

"No," Marina said. "And I think fifteen minutes? Let's just give it a bit."

"What if Mama comes to say good night?"

"It's not bedtime yet."

"What if Mama comes anyway?"

"I'm doing the best I can, Cordelia. Just give it a minute!"

They fell silent as they watched the greenish foam. They waited. They watched. Marina checked the clock on the nightstand beside Lir's bed. It had been about thirteen minutes, which was close enough. "Help me with the paper towels," she said.

The three of them started scrubbing *hard*. They put their whole bodies into it.

"It's working!" exclaimed Lir.

To Marina's surprise, it really was. The foam had pulled up the slime. They'd had to use almost an entire roll of paper towels (which Mama would have something to say about), but it was not as bad as a damaged rug. The rug would still need to dry. But at least it was a normal light-blue color again, not even a little green.

Lir squealed, jumping up and down before running headfirst at Marina for a hug. Cordelia joined in, and the two of them squeezed Marina around the middle so tightly she could barely breathe.

"Okay, okay. Get off me."

"I told you," Lir said. "I told you she'd help, Cordelia. Marina's the best!"

Marina blushed. Too bad the twins were too little to be her safety net tomorrow.

Still, it felt really good to be considered the best for once.

CHAPTER SEVENTEEN

The lagoon smelled like barbecue: charcoal, mixed with smoke, mixed with hot dogs and hamburgers.

The lagoon sounded like summer. Everyone was outside, and the motors of various boats were running, and Mom was calling over to Mr. Martin, who was calling over to Mr. Badger. A little way down the lagoon, Jamie Perez and her friends were blasting music. Above them, the seagulls cawed as they flew toward the marshes.

And the lagoon looked like heaven. Harbor and Sam and Cordelia and Lir and Pork and Sonny were in the water. The sun reflected off the surface, making them squint in the bright light. Sonny would have to pull the floaties out at the end of the night, but for now they were in the lagoon: an avocado, a flamingo, and a unicorn, all for the taking.

Marina stood inside the Ali-O'Connor house, watching and smelling and hearing everything, her stomach hurting worse and worse as the afternoon ticked by. They wouldn't be going out on the boats for the parade until after dinner, when the sun was starting to set, so that by the time they processed down the lagoon and across the bay, the lights would shine brightly in the darkness. But Marina would have to act now if she was going to go through with Boom's plan and put herself in fake danger. She checked the clock on the microwave in the kitchen. Boom hadn't come over yet.

There was a crash, and Marina saw that another part of Frankencrab had fallen to bits on the deck. She glared at it. If only Lir would take issue with *that* mess, just like the others Marina had to help clean up.

Mama came in through the back door, headed for the kitchen. "Hey, you. You coming outside with everyone?"

"In a minute."

"I'm just getting the corn ready," Mama said. She peered into the big pot of boiling water on the stove. She lowered the temperature and reached into the colander for the ears she had already shucked and washed. She dropped them gently, one by one, into the water.

"Can we throw away what's left of Frankencrab now?" Marina asked.

Mama laughed. "It'll end up falling apart on its own. Just leave it be."

"It's disgusting," Marina said. "I don't know why it's still even out there."

"We have this conversation like every other day, Marina."

"Yeah, we do. And it's still out there!"

Mama took one last glance at the corn in the pot. She wiped her hands on a dish towel and came over to stand by Marina. She wrapped her in a side hug that Marina didn't want. She didn't push Mama away, but she made a face.

"I can't just throw it away. It's important to Cordelia and Lir," Mama said.

Marina chose her next words very, very carefully. "What if it's important to me that you get rid of it?"

Mama laughed. Marina didn't know what was funny. "Just leave it alone. It makes your siblings happy, and that's what's important." Mama paused before exclaiming, "Oh, shoot! That reminds me, I forgot about the crab dip. I'll be right back." She ducked out of the room and through the door to the garage, where they had an extra refrigerator they used when their actual refrigerator ran out of room. They used the spare refrigerator often.

Marina watched her go with a scowl on her face. Of course the only important thing was that Cordelia and Lir were happy. Of course Marina's opinion and happiness didn't actually matter. With Mama out of the room, Marina decided to act. She didn't need Mama's permission. She crossed to the cabinet under the sink and pulled out a big garbage bag. She shook it out with a loud *swoosh*, which startled Good Boy.

Marina took that bag and stormed outside.

She didn't hesitate or detour. She marched right over to Frankencrab. She started with the broken bits all over the floor by Frankencrab's feet, shoving them as hard as she could into the bag. Once that was finished, she began tugging at the rest of it. She'd managed to pull off one of its eyes, which was made out of a bunch of empty shells, before anyone noticed.

"Hey!" It was Cordelia who shouted from the middle of the lagoon. "Hey! What are you doing? Marina! What are you doing to Frankencrab?"

Marina didn't stop.

She needed the entire thing to tumble over. She reached for the base of Frankencrab, the two bigger crab-shell legs that held him up, and she kicked one as hard as she possibly could. It broke apart immediately, and in one terrible, amazing, rumbling motion, the entire structure—the other leg, the rest of his arms and claw and body and head—came collapsing down. It landed in a crumbly heap, dust and crab bits floating into the air as seagulls swooped and cawed above Marina's head, eager to take a closer look.

The back deck got really, really quiet. And then Cordelia, who had climbed up the ladder and out of the lagoon with Lir right at her heels, started wailing.

Cordelia was crying full, strong little-kid cries, tears streaming down her cheeks, eyes closed tight, and she could barely catch her breath. She wasn't saying anything coherent. She just kept sobbing. Tears spilled over Lir's cheeks, too.

Mom, who was over near Mr. Martin's deck, chatting with him and Mr. Harris, came rushing over. She knelt down beside Cordelia, wrapping an arm around her. "What's going on?"

"What'd you do that for, Marina?" Harbor said as she pulled herself up the ladder.

Sam, Sonny, and Pork were watching quietly from the water. Cordelia wouldn't stop crying, taking shuddering, shallow breaths between sobs.

Mom looked from Cordelia to the heap of crab bits on the floor to Marina. "You did this?"

Marina had the garbage bag gripped tightly in her hands. This didn't feel good. Not like it was supposed to. Cordelia wouldn't calm down, and Marina hadn't wanted to hurt *her*. She was just so mad at Mama. "It was falling apart!" said Marina, trying to defend herself.

"Hey!" Mama came out through the back door.

Cordelia ran right into her arms, which made Marina's stomach hurt and her eyes fill with tears. She didn't want to cry, though, so she did what Harbor always did and clenched her teeth, hoping it would keep the tears from falling.

"I just told you to leave it alone, Marina," Mama said. "I *just told you* not to touch it!"

This wasn't good. They were hours away from the Parade of Lights. Marina had finally been making progress on being her family's favorite. Now, they were all looking at her as though she had done something really bad, like hurt Good Boy or burned the marshes down. Her entire family and Sonny and Pork Badger were looking at her like the opposite of how you'd look at your favorite anything.

"It was falling apart anyway," Marina said again, desperately. "I was just cleaning up the deck so it was nice and clean. For Mom!"

Mama hoisted Cordelia, who was still wailing, onto her hip as if she was four and not seven. She reached for the garbage bag in Marina's hand and tugged it away. "You didn't do this for Mom. You did it for yourself, which was selfish, Marina. Go inside, and wait for us to come talk to you."

"But—"

"Hey. Listen to your mama," Mom said. "Go inside."

Marina's chest felt tight. She needed to fix this. She needed Boom.

Without another word, Marina did as she was told. She went inside, leaving the rest of her family out back. She could hear Mom telling Harbor to help put the rest of Frankencrab in the garbage bag and Mama continuing to comfort Cordelia.

Marina did as she was told, but then she kept going. She went into the house and through the living room, and right to the front door. Good Boy followed at her heels, whining, wanting to go out. Marina ignored him, walking out of the house. Good Boy was left standing at the front door, watching her through the glass. Marina could still hear Cordelia crying. She could hear everyone else resuming their splashing in the bay. She could hear Jamie Perez's music.

And without hesitating, without anyone noticing, Marina walked straight to Boom's house.

Boom's mom answered the door. Half of her hair was straight; the other half was wavy and pulled up in a side ponytail. "Oh, hello, Mariana."

"Marina," Marina corrected. "Is Boom here?"

Boom's mom held the door open wider. "She's in her room. Go on up. I've gotta finish straightening my hair. I'm ridiculously late as is!" She rushed off, heading toward her own bedroom as Marina went to Boom's.

Boom had two bathing suits laid out on her bed. Marina knocked gently on her open door so she didn't startle her. Amato darted out from his place under Boom's bed to rub against Marina's legs. Boom glanced over her shoulder. "Oh! Good! You can help me pick. Since I've never been on a boat before. Which one is the best boat bathing suit?"

Marina was out of breath. "I thought you were coming over

today. To help me with the plan? We need to hurry. I think I messed up big-time. I think we need to do the plan now before anything goes worse."

Boom immediately abandoned her bathing suits. She grabbed her phone and held it up to Marina's face. "Tell me everything. Go."

"Everyone's mad at me. I don't have time to explain! Did you brainstorm? Did you come up with anything? We need to act now, Boom! My family doesn't even know I'm here right now."

Boom nodded once, firmly. "Okay. I was waiting for my mom to leave for her party. She was going to walk me over your house. But okay. I'll just tell her we're going now. But this is good—this works. My mom won't have any idea I'm actually gone."

"Actually gone where?" Marina asked.

"We're going to hide. Both of us. Me with the camera, so we get it recorded. And then your family will look for you. Probably."

"*Probably?*"

"Whoever likes you most will find you. They'll know where to look, and they'll notice you're missing first, and they'll come find you," Boom explained. "And then we'll know who your safety net is. Not that I think you actually need a safety net, for the record. Like, I'm really excited to go on the boat later, and I'm sure with your mom driving and everything, it'll all be fine. Great, even."

Marina picked up the purring cat at her feet. Amato leaned his entire body against hers, and Marina clung to the warmth of him. "Fine, yeah. Let's do your plan. But where do we hide?"

"I thought about that, too. I think we should go to that park you're always talking about. The one you always want to go to instead of anything water-related," Boom said, and Marina blushed a little. "If I was looking for you and you weren't at home, that's where I would look."

"Okay," Marina said.

"Okay?"

"Yes. Okay."

"Now?"

"Yes." Marina nodded. "Now."

They didn't waste any more time. Boom called to her mom, who was still working on her hair. "Mom, I'm going over to Marina's for the barbecue! And then the parade. On the boat. You can pick me up after your party!"

"Okay," Boom's mom called back. "Have fun! Behave yourself!"

Boom had her phone in one hand. She grabbed Marina's nice and tightly in the other as she tugged her out of the house. The two of them walked like that, hand in hand, up the street. They walked like that up two streets, around the corner, and all the way to the end of the block. There was the boat ramp, protected by a locked metal gate. All the adults on Sunrise Lagoon had a key.

That was fine. Marina didn't need the gate, or the boat ramp. Having the gate closed was like having extra protection, even. It was the park's safety net. The park was along the side of the boat ramp, starting at the end of the lagoon and the beginning of the wide-open bay. It was surrounded by pilings. When the Ali-O'Connor siblings were younger, their moms used to fret about them getting too close to the edge. Marina always stayed far away from that edge now. She made her way over to the swings, which were set far from the water, and tugged Boom along with her.

"Okay," Marina said. She started giggling. She wasn't sure why. "We're here. We made it. Now what?"

Boom sat on a swing and kicked her feet, picking up speed. Her phone camera was, as always, pointed directly at Marina.

"Now we wait."

CHAPTER EIGHTEEN

They waited. And waited. And waited.

And then they waited some more.

Boom was recording a spectacular view of the sky. The sun was getting lower, turning blues and pinks and purples. She was leaning back on the swing, pointing the phone up, and twisting the swing, around and around and around, before letting go and spinning like a wild top, making the colors of the setting sun swirl together. She said it would make really good B-roll, which, she explained, was the footage they used in films for background shots and things like that. Marina was pretty sure Boom was just bored.

"Why do you like this park so much?" Boom asked. "Wait—say it right into the camera."

Marina's cheeks flushed. "I don't. I mean, it's fine. It's just the easiest thing to convince my siblings to do instead of swimming in the bay or going on the boat. Cordelia and Lir like the monkey bars. Sometimes Sonny and Harbor go crabbing over there." She pointed. "I can stay back here, on the swings, minding my own business."

"That makes sense," Boom said.

There were some families using the grills and the picnic area set up along the grass. Later, they'd wave as the parade of bright and colorful boats drove by. Marina turned in her swing to look at the families, trying to spot Harbor or Sam or Mom, or *anybody*.

She huffed. "How long has it been?"

"Oh, shoot," Boom said. "I forgot to look at the time when we got here. Wait! Let me see how long I've been recording . . . Yeah, okay. I've been filming us for about seventeen minutes."

"This was a bad idea. No one's gonna come," Marina said. "They probably still think I'm in a time-out in my room. They're probably all still comforting Cordelia. Or rebuilding Frankencrab or something. We should just go back. Maybe they'll ground me and I won't be allowed to join the parade anyway."

"That'd be awful!" said Boom.

"Oh, it's fine. You can still go on the boat with the rest of my family."

"But, Marina, it wouldn't be the same without you," Boom said.

Behind them, a little kid started crying. Marina turned to

see a mom carrying her toddler. They were standing close to the pilings, looking out at the bay. The mom was trying to point out Barnegat Lighthouse, across the wide-open water. The toddler was kicking her chubby little legs, as if she was trying to run away, her little fists holding tight to her mom's shirt. "Don't be afraid," her mom was saying. "I've got you. You don't need to worry. Nothing will happen to you."

"Let's just go back," Marina said to Boom. "Let's just forget it and go home."

It filled Marina with incandescent rage when she and Boom approached the Ali-O'Connors' front door and they could hear everyone still on the deck. It sounded like the entire lagoon was there, hanging out and having fun—and not caring that Marina was at her wit's end.

"Well, we could at least go eat," Boom said, looking on the bright side. "It smells awesome, even from all the way out here."

Marina ignored her.

She opened the door and the minute the two of them stepped inside, Good Boy started barking and crying and whining his head off. He jumped onto Marina, who scolded him to get down, and then he ran over to his leash and bopped it with his nose.

"No one took you out yet?" Marina said, and then sighed. She scratched his head. "At least I'm not the only Ali-O'Connor everyone apparently forgot about." She sighed again. "Well, I'm not doing it. Come on. We'll go get Mom."

Good Boy led the way, running ahead and practically barreling into the back door as he barked nonstop. Marina, followed by Boom, walked over and opened it. Good Boy sped out of the house, still barking.

"Mom!" yelled Marina. "Good Boy is going absolutely bonkers. Can you just walk him already?"

Complete silence washed over the deck.

Even the seagulls seemed to go completely quiet.

Marina realized everyone was staring at her. Mom had her cell phone pressed against her ear, Harbor hovering closely next to her. Sam and the twins were wrapped in towels, sitting at the table. The Badgers—all of them, including George and their grandparents—were there, too. And Mr. Martin and Mr. Harris were standing next to them. Mr. Martin was the first person to speak: "Oh, thank god."

Then Mama came out of nowhere, stepped right in front of Marina, grabbed her by the shoulders, and held her there. Mama looked a bit like Amato did when Boom accidentally yelled in his face and he poofed up. "Where were you? Where in god's name have you been?" shrieked Mama, and then she pulled Marina into a crushing hug. Marina could barely breathe.

Mom came close, too. "I was on the phone with the police. We couldn't find you anywhere! You know all the rules!"

It took Marina a moment to catch up. Her head was spinning, and everyone—*everyone*—was still looking at her. "Oh," she said. "I guess you did notice I was gone."

"Of course we noticed! Where did you go? What were you *thinking*?"

"Excuse me," Boom interrupted, "but maybe, possibly, could you tell us who noticed first?"

"I'm sorry—*what*?" Mom said, her voice wobbly. Good Boy, who was still eager to go for a walk, kept bumping his head against her legs. It almost knocked her over.

"Hey, Boom," Sonny said from his spot at the table. "Maybe come over here. With us?"

"I went looking for you not even two minutes after you went inside," Mama said. She still had a tight grip on Marina, as if unwilling to let go. "I couldn't find you. Anywhere. It was like you just . . . Where were you?"

Marina couldn't answer her. Everyone was staring at her, and her chest felt really tight, and her stomach hurt, and she didn't know where to begin. "I don't know," she said.

"What do you mean, you don't know?"

"Explain. *Now*, Marina," Mom said.

"I can't," Marina said, now breathing a little funny. "I can't!"

"I can!" shouted Boom.

"Boom, stop!" yelled Harbor from her place behind Mom.

And then Marina's voice started coming out of Boom's cell phone.

"*I'm the* last *one anyone would think about saving. You'll see. Sam and Harbor are Mom's favorites, because they love the boats. Plus, Harbor was here first. And Mama has the twins. She wanted to have them more than anything, you know. Even though they'd already adopted me.*"

The deck was quiet again as everyone listened. Mama began asking a question, but she cut herself short as the recording kept playing.

"*You're smack-dab in the middle,*" Boom's voice said, coming through the cell phone.

And then Marina's again: "*I wasn't supposed to be. But then came Sam.*"

Boom turned that video off. "Wait, hang on. That wasn't the right one. Let me find it."

"What is that?" Mom asked. "What are you—"

"Here! This one," Boom said, and she pushed PLAY.

"*Why are you filming me?*" Marina's voice said. Marina wanted to reach over and yank the phone out of Boom's hand. She wanted to throw it in the water and destroy it. She wanted to go back in time before everyone on the deck could hear what she had said.

She couldn't, though. She couldn't take her eyes off Mama.

Boom's voice came from the recording now. "*Reaction shots. I was thinking about what you said about boat accidents and* Jaws *and stuff. Actually, it gave me nightmares, so thanks for that. But! What if I could guarantee that someone would make sure you were safe if anything happened? Wouldn't that make you feel a little better about going on the boats?"*

"Um . . . Well, I guess. But how?"

"We just make sure you're someone's favorite. Then you'd be the first one they'd protect. Like, if Amato and a regular cat were both on the roof of the house for some reason, I'd be waiting on the ground as Amato's safety net. I mean, I'd be worried about the other cat, too, but Amato is my favorite everything.*"*

"But I already told you—I'm not anyone's favorite anything.*"*

Mama didn't move as she listened to the recorded conversation from what seemed to Marina like ages ago. Mama was frozen, like a statue. Like Frankencrab before Marina had torn him down. And then Mama blinked, and her eyes filled up, and Marina's stomach hurt even more.

"Boom, give me that," Mom said, taking Boom's phone from her without waiting. She started scrolling through it, through all the recordings they had made for Boom's documentary.

Mr. Martin suddenly came up behind Marina, which startled her. Some part of her was aware that everyone was still watching her, but she'd also felt like she and her moms and Boom (and Boom's phone) were the only ones there. "Okay, I think we should give Miss Marina and her moms some space here," Mr. Martin said. "The rest of you Ali-O'Connors, come on over to my yard. Me and Mr. Harris here will keep an eye on ya."

Mr. Harris was already scooping Cordelia up and onto his shoulders, even though she was much too big and he was much too old for it, and the Badgers were gathering themselves to go back to their house. Boom hesitated, unsure where she was supposed to go. Good Boy whined.

"Harbor, take Good Boy out first, please," Mom said, using her no-nonsense voice. "Boom, go ahead with Mr. Harris and Mr. Martin. I'm going to just hold on to your phone for a bit, and then I'll give it back."

Everyone dispersed. Harbor, Sam, Lir, Cordelia, and Boom looked Marina's way before heading over to Mr. Martin's.

Mom hit PLAY on Boom's phone, and Marina's voice started up again, saying, "*And maybe things went pretty well with Harbor and Sam and Mom, but I don't know for sure if I'm anyone's favorite. I still don't know if I'd have a safety net.*"

"*We need to run a test. Remember I said so? It was right before we fought, so maybe you don't. We need to put you in fake peril so we can see who would come save you.*"

"*That sounds dangerous.*"

Mom pressed STOP and put the phone in her back pocket. She rubbed her face. "Okay. Okay, I'm going to ask you a question, Marina, and I need you to answer it as honestly as possible. Okay?"

Marina nodded her head. She used her shoulder to slowly wiggle her way out of Mama's grasp. Mama let go.

"I'm a little confused. But it sounds like you and Boom were trying to do some sort of . . . plan. Is that right?" Mom said.

Marina glanced over at Mr. Martin's yard. All her siblings were still looking in her direction. "Yeah."

"I need you to explain that plan to us."

"Well, Boom thought . . . and I guess it was partly my idea, too. Maybe. But it was mostly Boom, because I didn't actually think it would work. And I guess it didn't. So I was right anyway."

"*Marina.*"

"I didn't want to go on the boat for the Parade of Lights, but I didn't want to keep talking about it, either, so I promised you I would, and I knew I had to try and go, but I was afraid that if something bad happened I wouldn't have a safety net. I need a safety net. Did you know that over two thousand people get injured in boating accidents a year? I think I told you that. I *did* tell you that. So Boom said if I made sure someone would definitely be that safety net for me—like if I was stuck on a roof they'd be the one to stand below and make sure if I fell they'd catch me—I'd feel safe enough to go on the boat." Marina was out of breath when she was done explaining. "Oh. And we were at the park. We were waiting to see who would come get me first, because whoever that was would probably be the one to catch me in the roof example."

Her moms just stared at her silently. Mom clenched her teeth, like Harbor sometimes did. Mama's eyes were wet. They looked at each other and then back at Marina. Mom took a deep breath. "Okay. That's . . . a lot to unpack. I knew you were afraid of the boats, and maybe I should have taken that more seriously. You've been a little ball of anxiety lately, and your mama and I want to help you figure that out. But, Marina, if this all stems from you being afraid that neither of us would do everything we could to keep you safe . . . we've talked about that. Of *course* we would keep you safe. Both of us. Always."

Marina tried not to sigh or roll her eyes, or do anything else that would set Mom off. She looked over at Mama instead.

Mama blinked, and a tear spilled from her eye. Marina watched it as it rolled over her cheek and down her chin, where it hovered before Mama reached up to wipe it away. "You said something. In the video," Mama said. "You said that I love the twins more than anything, because I wanted them more than anything, even though we adopted you."

Marina looked away.

"What did you mean by that?" Mama asked.

A seagull swooped down to hop along the deck. Marina watched it as it went toward the pile of crab shells that used to be Frankencrab. Some of them had been picked up since Marina had left, but most of them were just lying there. Marina tried to take a deep breath, but it got caught in her lungs. Her stomach hurt so bad. Everything burned a little, and she suddenly wanted everyone around her to burn, too. "You love the twins the most, and I hate you for it!" she yelled. "You had *me*, you adopted *me*, but you didn't want me, because you wanted them! You wanted to have them, like Mom had Harbor, even though you both had me!"

"Oh my god, that's why you've been so weird with Mama lately," Mom said softly, almost like she was whispering it to herself. She added, louder, "Marina, that's not true. That's . . . Okay. We need to be better about this. Your mama and I need to be better about talking to you kids and *listening* to you and really hearing you. I love our family. I love how it came together. I love that Mama took me and Harbor into her heart when we first met her, and I love that we decided to adopt you. You were perfect. You *are* perfect."

"Then why did—"

"We wanted a big family. We wanted this beautiful, big family. So we knew we wanted more, and Mama and I talked a long time about how we wanted to do that. And, honestly Marina? There was a really long waiting list at the adoption agency, and Mama had a physical scheduled, and her doctor said she was healthy but she *was* getting older, so that if we wanted to, it was a good time." Mama shrugged. "So we did. And then we found Sam. And I looked at Sam, just like I looked at Harbor and you and the twins in the hospital right after you were born, and I knew she was a piece of my heart, too. Do you understand what I'm saying?"

Marina's chest loosened a little, even though her stomach still ached something wicked. "I don't know."

Mom looked over Marina's head at Mama. "Hon?"

Mama broke. That was the best way that Marina could explain it. One minute she was just standing there, and the next her entire face had crumbled, and she folded up, and she crouched right down to her knees, so she was eye to eye with Marina—even if Mama's eyes were full of tears and she probably couldn't see Marina all that clearly. She put her hands on Marina's cheeks, and they were warm, and Marina didn't pull away.

"I love you so much. I'm so sorry I ever made you feel like I didn't. Or that I could love anyone more than you. I love you all so much. I love you so much." Mama's hands moved to Marina's arms, holding tightly. "I'm so sorry. Tell me what you need."

Marina didn't know what to say to that. This wasn't exactly going how she'd thought it would. She'd thought they would yell and yell, and then it would be time to go on the boat, and Marina would hyperventilate the entire time.

She had no idea what she needed. "I don't know," she said again.

"Do you believe me?" Mama asked.

Marina swallowed. It felt like rocks going down her throat. "I don't know."

"Okay," Mom said, cutting in, and Marina was relieved. "Okay, here's what we're going to do. We're going to keep talking about this, right? With you, and the entire family. Sam had some pretty big feelings about being adopted earlier this summer, and I'm hearing *you* now, Marina. And I'm sure Harbor sometimes has big feelings, and Lir told me recently that sometimes the two of you talk about how it gets hard to breathe when things go a little wonky, right? So we all have a lot to talk about. And we're going to do that together, and we're going to do that with a counselor."

"I don't want to see a counselor!"

"I want you to talk to Sam about it," Mom said. "She sees her counselor twice a month, and she can tell you how she feels about it. So just listen to what she has to say. Okay?"

Marina slowly nodded, and the three of them fell quiet. It was the kind of quiet where it felt like someone should probably say something—Marina felt like she should say something—but no one knew what it should be. A sudden crackle made Marina jump, and she looked across the lagoon. The Badger boys and their grandfather had turned their boat on and flipped the switch. All the lights that they had strung were lit up, bright and beautiful. It looked like a pirate ship, with glowing lights along the masts and at the front and on fake cannons along the sides.

Sonny, Pork, and their grandfather were cheering. George didn't cheer, the grumpy teenager that he was, but he *was* smiling.

Behind them, Mr. Martin shouted for Mr. Harris to do the honors. His boat lit up, too. It looked like it was on fire. Since the lights were bright reds and oranges and yellows, Marina assumed that was the point.

"What do we do now?" Marina asked, looking at *Harbor Me*, floating next to the dock, unlit and covered with shadows.

CHAPTER NINETEEN

Their moms called everyone home and inside. Including Boom, who admitted she'd lied to her mom and *said* she'd told the Ali-O'Connors her mom would be at a party that night, even though she hadn't. They all sat in the living room. Boom and Marina shared one of the couches, while Cordelia and Lir wiggled nervously on the other. Harbor slouched in the lounge chair, while Sam sat on the floor with Good Boy.

Marina watched the sun set lower and lower through the windows, the sky growing dark.

"We're going to sit the parade out this year," Mom said, answering the question on everyone's minds.

No one said anything. Not Harbor, who looked like she might burst into tears. Not Cordelia or Lir, who kept sending anxious glances toward Marina.

Sam turned to look at Marina, too, and Marina wondered again if Sam ever thought about her birth family. If she ever thought about what it would be like to still live with them. If thinking about that ever made Sam's stomach feel full of rocks. She wondered what Sam talked to her counselor about, and if she ever talked about Marina.

Boom heaved a big sigh next to Marina. She still hadn't gotten her phone back from Mom, and Marina knew Boom wanted to make a documentary to impress her dad. She also knew Boom wanted to go on the boat tonight more than anything.

But the summer was nearly over, and Marina was still scared.

Maybe that was why she said it. Or maybe she just was tired of feeling so weird, of feeling like it was hard to breathe and her stomach would never stop hurting. She wanted Mom and Mama to do something to take the weirdness away. They had listened to her, and she had listened to them, but still everything felt wrong. Nothing felt good. Marina just wanted *something* to finally feel good.

Maybe that was why Marina suddenly said, "I want to do the parade."

Her moms exchanged glances. "I don't know about that, little fish," Mom said.

Marina focused on Mama. "You said to tell you what I need. This is what I need. Okay? So can we just get this over with?"

Marina's palms were already starting to sweat. She wiped them on her shorts.

Her moms exchanged glances again.

"I don't know," Mom said. "Are you sure?"

Marina looked at the rest of her family. They were all sitting on the edges of their seats, eagerly waiting for the answer. Boom was practically buzzing next to her, trying, and failing, to hold back a giant smile.

Marina was pretty sure she might regret this. She was also sure she couldn't let the summer end without doing it. "Yeah. Whatever. I'm sure."

They boarded *Harbor Me* one by one. The Badgers were pulling their boat away from the dock, and Mr. Martin and Mr. Harris were already on their way up the lagoon. The Perezes' boat had about thirty teenagers hanging off it, blasting music as they got ready to go. The sun had almost disappeared, and the sky was turning shades of dark purple. The Ali-O'Connors had to scramble to get ready to join the parade.

Good Boy wasn't pleased about being left behind, but Mom didn't like bringing him on the boat at night. As it was, Mom always got a little on edge when she took them out in the dark, so she kept going over the rules again and again. "Rules are important! But the rules are great. They're so we're safe. Which we will be!"

Which didn't really fill Marina with the confidence Mom had apparently thought it would.

Marina and Boom were the last to get on the boat. "You go first," Marina said.

Mom pulled the boat close and held out a hand. "Just hold on to me, and hop right on. Marina's mama is right on the other side—she'll help steady you. Okay?"

Boom took a deep breath, nodded her head once, and did exactly as she was told.

And then it was Marina's turn. She felt like she might start crying, but she was determined to do this. She had to just . . . do this.

"You ready, little fish?" Mom asked.

"I think so."

"You think so?"

"No. I mean, I am." Marina nodded, just like Boom had. "I am."

Marina held her breath, held tightly on to Mom's hands, and jumped onto the boat like she had done a million times, since as long as she could remember. She had done this last summer, and the summer before that, and the summer before that. She had done this her entire life.

She held on to Mom's hand until Mama's arms wrapped around Marina's middle. She let Mama cling to her a moment, leaning into the touch.

And then Mom called out for Harbor and Sam to start untying the ropes. Cordelia and Lir started chanting—"Turn on the lights! Turn on the lights! Turn on the lights!"—and Mom pushed the buttons that set *Harbor Me* aglow, sparkling with white and rainbow lights. Everyone cheered.

The boat jerked forward, and Boom, who was sitting with the twins, reached out to hold on to Cordelia's life vest.

"Okay, everyone take a seat. And no one move! Where you're sitting is where you sit. No swapping. No standing. Boom, you listening? That's your seat," Mom said. "Marina, where do you want to go?"

Back in bed, preferably. "Um."

"Mama needs to sit with the twins. But just because they're too little to sit by themselves! Right? And I need to drive. So do you want to sit next to me?" Mom said. She seemed a little more frazzled than usual, and it made Marina's stomach hurt.

"Um," Marina said again.

"Okay. How about this. Cordelia, you come next to me. Mama will squish herself right between Marina and Lir, and Marina can also sit next to Boom," Mom said, deciding for everyone.

They took their seats, and the Ali-O'Connors, plus Boom, joined the Parade of Lights.

The boats of Sunrise Lagoon, lit up and spectacular, met up with all the other boats out on the bay. There was a boat decorated in pinks and purples with giant peace signs. Mr. Martin's boat was wrapped up in blue, with white lights to make teeth, which looked like a giant shark gliding above the water. There was a tropical-inspired boat with brightly lit green palm trees, and another that looked like a train, chugging its way into the bay. Neighbors and friends who weren't actually in the parade were on their decks or in the park, waving and cheering.

Mom called over to the other boats with compliments, and then followed those up by telling the kids how much better the Ali-O'Connor decorations were. Lir asked if Mom could turn on the radio, and she turned it up nice and loud. Harbor had Sonny on a video call, so it was like they were together. Cordelia was shouting out which boats were her favorites, changing her mind every two seconds. Once Sam had permission, she went to sit in Mom's seat—the captain's seat—and steered the boat with Mom close behind her, hand on the wheel along with Sam's.

Boom had big, wide eyes and didn't say a thing. She was quieter than Marina had ever seen her. She seemed too busy to talk, taking in the boats, the water, and the parade. And even though she had gotten her phone back from Mom, she wasn't recording anything.

Marina just tried to breathe normally.

She tried not to think about boating accidents and electrical fires and pirates and *Jaws*. She tried not to think about what would happen if the boats in the parade got too close to one another and couldn't stop and crashed.

Boom reached out to hold Marina's hand and swung their arms back and forth. "This is so cool," Boom whispered. Marina didn't even know Boom *could* whisper.

It reminded Marina of when Sam had come to live with them and she was in awe of the shiny, sparkly boats. Marina *must* have felt that way once, too. She wished she could remember that feeling.

Mama wrapped an arm around Marina, holding her tight. "I've got you," she said. "Don't worry about the water. Look at all the lights. Tell me your favorite."

"Mine is the train," Cordelia called out. "Or the crocodile!"

"It's an alligator," Harbor said. "I like the train, too."

Lir answered next. "I like the pirate ship!"

"I like the tropical one, I think," Sam said. "Or maybe the shark."

Mom laughed. "Why aren't any of you picking ours?"

"I like yours, Mrs. Ali-O'Connor," Boom said.

"Thank you, Boom."

"But, I mean, I really like the shark best," Boom added.

Mom groaned.

Mama squeezed Marina's arm. "All right, Marina. How about you? Which one do you like best?"

Marina carefully craned her head to look ahead of them, at all the brightly lit boats. The lighthouse shone in the distance, and if Marina squinted to look behind her, she could even see their house on the lagoon. She looked at the green palm trees and the purple peace signs and the blue fin of the shark. She looked at the red caboose of the train, and the white sail of the

Badger family's pirate ship. She looked at the rainbow waterfall on *Harbor Me*.

Marina looked at the boats and then back into Mama's eyes.

"I don't know. I like all of them," Marina said, leaning into Mama. "I don't have a favorite."

They arrived back at their house in Sunrise Lagoon after bedtime. Like on the Fourth of July, they were allowed to stay up late. Mom made a fire in the firepit to roast marshmallows, and Jamie Perez and her friends started shooting off the leftover fireworks from the other day, to the pleading and cheers of Cordelia, Lir, and Pork.

But it also wasn't like the Fourth of July, when summer was in full swing, when it felt like it would never end. Now, school was less than three days away. Summer *was* ending.

Marina felt ready for bed. She sat next to Boom as Boom made and ate three s'mores, but Marina didn't want any. Her stomach was still too queasy. She didn't say anything about that, though. She had done her best to avoid her moms since climbing off the boat. She didn't even want to look at them, afraid making eye contact would start a conversation she was too tired to have.

Mr. Martin and Mr. Harris came by to say good night. Mr. Martin squeezed Marina's shoulder and waited until she looked up at him before saying, "Don't go scaring us like that again. Don't know what we'd do without our poker buddy."

When he walked away, Boom bumped Marina's shoulder. "See? *He* likes you best, I think."

Marina shrugged.

"*I* like you best, too," Boom said. "Just, you know, so you know. I'd be your safety net."

Marina smiled at her. It made her stomach hurt a little less. "Thanks, Boom. I'd be your safety net, too."

Soon, Boom's mom came to pick her up, and after Marina's moms had a long conversation with her about everything that had happened, it was, finally, bedtime. Marina was relieved. She was absolutely exhausted, and all she wanted was to forget about the entire day and just go to sleep. She brushed her teeth and climbed into bed and mumbled good nights to her moms when they came to tuck them in. They hovered a bit, but neither tried to start a conversation. Marina figured that would happen soon—probably tomorrow—but she was grateful to have avoided it for now.

Marina rolled over, about to turn her sound machine on, but before she could, she heard Harbor say, "Um, Marina?"

Marina looked up to find Harbor and Sam sitting up and staring at her. "Yeah?"

"We just . . . well . . ." Harbor fiddled with her bedsheet. "Did you only want to watch basketball with me because of the whole thing with Boom?"

Great, Marina thought. Now she was going to hurt Harbor's feelings. "I mean, I guess. Yeah." She glanced up at Diana Taurasi and cringed. Hopefully, she wouldn't come alive and avenge Harbor's honor or something.

"It's just, well, you didn't have to do that," Harbor said. "Like, you don't have to watch if you don't like it. I wouldn't let anything happen to you just because you didn't like basketball."

Marina felt her cheeks flush. "Oh."

"And I know I'm not a great swimmer, but I've been practicing a lot," Sam chimed in. "I would help you, too. But, well"—she paused, as if she wasn't sure she was going to continue—"I sometimes think about being different, too. Like you said to Boom, about being adopted? Mom and I talk about it sometimes. We can talk about it more together, too, if you want."

Marina could barely see their faces with the lights off. But there was something that felt safe about quietly confiding to her sisters in their dark bedroom. "Do you ever . . . think about your birth mom?" she asked Sam. "About what it was like to live with her."

"Sometimes," Sam admitted quietly. "Do you?"

"Sometimes." Marina glanced over at Harbor. "Sorry."

Harbor shrugged. "It's okay. I mean, I guess I'm sorry, too. I don't know what that's like. It must be weird. But . . . what you said about Mama? About the twins? I think about things like that, too, sometimes."

Marina was shocked. "You do?"

"When I go visit my dad, he always calls Mama my step-mom. It makes it sound less . . . real, I guess. Like that she's entirely your mom, but she's my *step*mom," Harbor said.

"I did like watching basketball with you. I didn't really understand it all. But I did like watching." Marina hesitated before adding, "Diana Taurasi scares me a little, though. I'd like you to take that poster down."

"Too bad," Harbor said. "I love her."

"Hey, Marina," Sam said. "Why are you suddenly afraid of the boats? You didn't used to be. I remember when I first came here, you and Harbor hopped onto the boats like it was noth-ing. I thought I'd never be able to catch up."

Marina thought really hard. "I don't know. I can't remem-ber. I loved the boats and the water, and it was only me and Harbor, and then the twins when they were babies had to learn to swim, and then you came and had to learn to swim, too, and everything kept changing, and I guess maybe I changed, too."

"I think that's okay," Sam said. "I think it's okay to not like the boats."

Marina didn't believe that. The Ali-O'Connors *were* their boats. They were this house on the lagoon. They were the splashes they made when they jumped off the dock. They were the wake left behind when mom drove fast. They were the bay and the beach and the birds and all of it. "Sam?" she said. "Do you like talking to your counselor?"

Sam hesitated. "She's okay. She's nice. I like that I can tell her whatever I'm thinking. And, when I'm too nervous to talk to our moms about like, my birth mom, or my grandma, I can talk to her about it. I like that she listens. Sometimes I don't want to talk, and she doesn't make me. It's okay."

"Why?" Harbor asked Marina. "Do you want to see a therapist, too?"

"Mama wants me to."

"Oh."

"Can we just go to sleep now?" Marina asked.

"Yeah. Okay."

"Good night, Marina."

Marina rolled over in bed, closed her eyes, and fell asleep.

CHAPTER TWENTY

Marina wasn't the last one to wake up the next morning. She wasn't sleeping late. No one ever actually slept late. Good Boy was always loud, his nails clackety-clacking on the wood floors as he paced anxiously, wanting someone to take him out. Cordelia and Lir were even louder. Plus, Marina shared a very small bedroom with *two* of her sisters.

So, no, she wasn't the last one awake. She wasn't sleeping in. She was lying in bed, *pretending*.

She was about to surrender and climb out of bed when there was a knock on door. Mama stuck her head in. "Hey. Put some pants on quick. I'm gonna take Good Boy for a long walk to stretch his legs. I'd like you to maybe join me. If that sounds okay?"

"I guess so."

"You don't have to."

"Okay."

"Okay, you will? Or okay, you won't?"

Marina's head was spinning. Things with Mama weren't normally this confusing. Mom might be always the one to discipline them, but Mama was the parent who always had things under control. She didn't sound like she had everything under control right now, and that made Marina's stomach clench. "Okay, I will," she said.

Mama looked relieved. Marina didn't like that much, either. "Oh, good. Okay. Meet me outside the front door when you're ready."

Marina swapped her pajamas for sweatpants. She didn't bother brushing her teeth. She didn't brush her hair, either, just chucked it up in a giant bun. Her flip-flops still weren't by the front door—she hadn't found them yet, and had been rotating between her siblings'. This time, she ended up with Lir's, which were much too small.

Mama and Good Boy were, indeed, waiting outside the door. The sun was bright, and Marina had to shade her eyes and squint to see them. "Ready to go?" Mama said. Marina nodded and took her place beside her as Good Boy led the way.

They walked quietly at first. Good Boy pulled them to the edge of the marshes, sniffing (and occasionally biting) the tall grass. Mama had to keep tugging his leash to keep him from eating things he wasn't supposed to. The blue herons were out, two of them, and they looked so much larger than they had at the start of summer. Marina wondered if she looked larger to them, too, or if, instead, the herons thought she had shrunk as they got bigger and she stayed exactly the same.

She did feel a little taller. She noticed while walking next to Mama. She used to have to stand on her tiptoes to wrap her arms around Mama for a hug. Now, she'd be able to rest her head on Mama's shoulder with her feet flat on the ground.

"Did you get a chance to ask Sam about her counselor?" Mama finally said.

"Yeah. She said she's okay. She said she likes it fine."

"Did you think any more about that?"

Marina shrugged. "I don't think I like talking about things. But Sam also said her counselor doesn't make her talk if she doesn't want to. So . . . I don't know. Do I have to? When do I need to decide by?"

"Mom and I were thinking the three of us could go together. We thought it might be easier to talk with someone else's help," Mama said. "I'd really like to talk to you."

"We're talking now."

"We are."

"If I talk to you now, could we just leave it alone? We can just talk now, right? Let's do that. Let's just do that. So, what do you want to talk about, then? About Boom's documentary? Because that really was her idea. I think she misses her dad a lot. I think it helps her maybe not miss him so much when she has her camera recording," Marina explained. "Or did you want to talk about the boats? Because I did the parade last night, and that was fine, I guess. But I don't know. I guess I don't want to be afraid of the boats. I don't want you all to keep leaving me behind. But would a counselor be able to get me back on a boat again? It's not like she can change the statistics, Mama. Two thousand injuries is still a lot of injuries."

"Marina . . ."

"Or did you want to talk about the fact that I'm adopted?"

"All of it," Mama said, sounding slightly out of breath, even though Good Boy wasn't moving. He was staring, ears perked, at an egret who kept creeping closer instead of flying away. "I want to talk about all of it. Everything."

"Okay, fine."

"You're already getting annoyed with me."

"I'm not!" said Marina, annoyed.

"I love you, and I'm scared I'm pushing you away, and I don't really know why or how to fix that," Mama blurted out, loudly. It seemed to echo over the marshlands, and the egret Good Boy was stalking lifted its large white wings and few away. "Now your turn," Mama said to Marina.

Good Boy tugged on his leash, ready to move on. Mama let him pull her down the street.

Marina followed them. "I'm scared of being lost in the middle. Of Mom and Harbor and Sam. Of you and Cordelia and Lir. And I guess I don't know how to fix that." Marina paused before adding, "Your turn again."

"Mom and I read a million books before we adopted you. *And* Sam. And we took a bunch of classes. I thought I'd recognize the signs. I thought I'd never make the mistakes the moms in those books did," Mama said. "I was wrong, and that scares me, too. I didn't know you thought I had the twins because you weren't enough. That's . . . Marina, that's so far from the truth."

"My turn?"

"Yeah, your turn."

"Sometimes I think about how I'm part-Mexican and no one else is, and how I don't know anything about being Mexican, and that makes me feel weird and different, too."

"I understand a little, because I had my mom—your grandma—but I'm only half-Syrian, and sometimes I don't feel white enough *or* Syrian enough. I'm sorry I haven't tried talking to you about that part of who you are before. And I promise to talk you more about that. Your turn."

"I want to be someone's favorite. Your turn."

"Sometimes I want to be everyone's favorite. Favorite mom, I mean. Especially in the summer, when Mom is the fun one who drives the boat. Don't tell her I said that, though. Your turn."

"I don't have a favorite mom. I mean, I guess I like whichever one of you isn't bugging me at the time, but that's not always. That's just sometimes," Marina explained. "And it rotates, so it's both of you. Also, sometimes I think about the fact that I have three moms, really, if you think about it, and that feels a little weird, too."

"What feels weird about it?"

"It's your turn now."

"I wonder about your birth mom sometimes, too. I wonder if you have her eyes or nose, if she talks really, really fast and dances along to every little beat like you do. I wonder if you'll want to find her someday, and I wonder if I'll have been a good enough mom that you'll know that's perfectly okay. That she's part of you, and I wouldn't ever keep you from her, if you wanted to know more."

They reached the end of Sunrise Lagoon, the dead end where the bay began. They looked out at the water, watching the boats. A seagull was picking at a crab nearby, and Good Boy was barking at both the bird and its prey.

"I love being an Ali-O'Connor," Marina said. "I don't want anyone to think I don't, just because sometimes I think about my birth parents and because I don't like to go on the boats."

"We'd never think that," Mama said. "Never."

"I'm sorry if I hurt your feelings. I didn't do it on purpose. I don't know why I've been so mean to you," Marina said.

"I'm sorry if I hurt your feelings, because you thought I wanted the twins more than you. Or if you think I favor them. I didn't mean to ever make you feel that way," Mama said.

Good Boy barked again, but this time at Mama and Marina. He was ready to go back home. Neither of them moved, though. They looked at each other carefully, each of them wondering if they were ready to go home, too.

"So . . . are we okay?" Marina asked.

"I'd like to be," Mama said.

"Well, can we be?"

"Maybe . . . a work in progress," Mama suggested. "We can keep being honest with each other. *And* see a counselor to help us talk more. And go from there. Does that sound okay? Do you think we can do that?"

Marina still wasn't sure about talking to a counselor. But she felt better than she had in a while, here, talking to Mama. Her stomach didn't hurt at all.

"Okay. I guess we can try."

Mom met them at the front door when they returned home. Good Boy nearly knocked her over, excitedly anticipating his treat. "Don't come out back yet," Mom said, blocking the way.

"What? Why?" Marina asked.

"Just give me one more minute," Mom said, and then she disappeared through the house and out the back door.

Mama and Marina had just barely given Good Boy his treat and kicked off their shoes before Mom came back inside. She was slightly out of breath. "Okay, so I was thinking, you know, school starts on Tuesday, and then you'll end up having after-school activities and playdates and homework and all that noise. I'm not ready for that. I want us to enjoy one last really great summer day together. Today, I mean."

Great, Marina thought. Both of her moms were acting weird this morning.

Marina slumped her shoulders. "So we're going on the boat again, aren't we?" She really didn't want to do that. Her arms and legs felt tingly just thinking about it. It had barely been any time at all since she'd gone on the boat last night. But of course that was how Mom would want to spend their last summer day as a family. That was what Ali-O'Connors did in the summer. They went on the boats.

"Actually, no," Mom said. She had a big smile on her face that made Marina nervous. "So why don't you go get dressed and meet us out back, okay?"

Marina got dressed slowly, but there was only so much time she could waste before she would have to face the inevitable and go see whatever it was that her mom was up to. The house was quiet, which meant that her siblings were already outside.

She took so long that Mom sent Cordelia and Lir to get her. They knocked on her door and stuck their heads in, one on top of the other. Neither one of them said anything, and Marina realized they were looking at her kind of nervously. It brought a really vivid memory to Marina's mind: of Cordelia crying as Frankencrab tumbled down.

"Mom wanted us to check on you," Lir said.

"Okay."

"She wants you to come outside."

"I'm coming."

They quickly ducked out the door, and Marina sighed, feeling guilty. "Wait, come here," she called after them.

One after the other, they stuck their heads back through the doorway.

"I'm sorry about Frankencrab," Marina said.

The twins looked at each other before Cordelia asked, "Why were you so mad at me?"

"I wasn't mad at you. I was mad at Mama."

"Why?"

"It's a long story. But I wasn't mad at you. Or maybe I was a little, but it wasn't your fault. And anyway, I'm sorry. Okay?"

"Hang on," Cordelia said, and then she and Lir shut the door. Marina stared at it for a moment, wondering if she was supposed to follow them or something, but then the door opened up again.

This time, Cordelia and Lir came to stand inside the bedroom. "We decided that it's okay," Cordelia said. "But on one condition!"

"What's the condition?" Marina asked warily.

"You have to help me and Cordelia with our next project. Whatever it is. To make up for destroying Frankencrab," Lir said.

"Fine," Marina said.

"It's going to be even bigger and even better than Frankencrab, and you have to help, no matter what, and you cannot destroy it this time!" yelled Cordelia. "Promise!"

"I promise," Marina said. "Like, really. I promise. I'm sorry."

The twins looked at each other again, nodded their heads, and then reached out to each take one of Marina's hands. They pulled her. "Come on, then. Mom's waiting."

Marina let them tug her out of her bedroom, through the house, and out the back door. She'd expected her family to be gathered in the water or on a boat. Instead, though, they were all sitting around the long patio table. Everyone: her siblings, her moms, Mr. Harris and Mr. Martin, even Ms. Stewart from up the lagoon. Mr. Harris was shuffling a deck of cards. Mom was handing out little plastic poker chips, and Mama was pouring tall glasses of lemonade.

"Um," Marina said.

"Great! There you are," Mom said. "So we figured since we've mostly done the boats and fishing and things that the rest of us like to do all summer, we'd spend the day doing something you like to do. Mr. Martin says you're getting mighty good at taking all their money. I have to tell you, I'm a pretty good poker player myself."

"You have to teach us how to play, though," Harbor called. "I taught you basketball, so it's only fair!"

Marina didn't move from her spot.

"What do you think?" Mama said.

Marina glanced around the table. Mr. Harris was showing Sam how to shuffle a deck of cards, and Ms. Stewart was trying to explain some of the rules to Harbor. Mama took a seat next to them, wanting to listen to the rules, too. Cordelia and

Lir were at the edge of the deck with the fish net, scooping at something along the sides of the dock. Marina didn't even want to know what they were after. She could only assume that whatever it was, she would be helping them make some sort of bizarre sculpture out of it soon. A large black loon swooped down into the water, getting Good Boy's attention. He ran up and down the deck, barking his head off.

Across the way, Boom's back door swung open so hard it hit the wall of her house, echoing up the lagoon. "Marina! Hi! Hang on! I'll be right over!" she shouted, even though she didn't need to shout at all.

The sun shone brightly above them, high in the sky, as if summer wasn't about to end.

"I think," Marina said, smiling up at Mom as she finally answered her question, "I'm going to win."

CHAPTER TWENTY-ONE

The Ali-O'Connors were back on the deck the next morning, saying an official goodbye to summer. That was what it felt like anyway. Sam stood at the edge of the dock with a small Ugly Stik in her hand, one of Mom's old fishing rods, trying one last time to catch the little fish that had been jumping in the lagoon all morning.

Harbor was clenching her jaw, though it didn't do anything to stop the tears from spilling down her cheeks as she and Sonny stood in front of each other. They wouldn't hug. They used to, when they were little, but now they kind of just moped in solidarity as they said their goodbyes. Sonny kept glancing over at Sam, and Marina was pretty sure he didn't want to have to say goodbye to her, either.

Pork and the twins had somehow ended up in the lagoon, splashing around while Pork's mom yelled at him to get out and get dry. She didn't want him sitting in her car in his wet bathing suit, soaking through the seat.

"I got one," Sam called out. Harbor and Sonny ran over to her, Sonny grabbing the net as Sam reeled in her fish. It was a little one with a long, pointed nose. Sonny scooped it up.

"Put it back!" yelled Cordelia from the water.

"Don't let it die!" wailed Lir right after her.

Mom jogged over to help Sam release the fish back into the lagoon. It flopped in, the water rippling in little circles before it swam away.

Boom stood next to Marina, holding up her phone to film everyone. "This is kind of depressing," Boom said.

"The end of the summer is always sad," Marina said.

"Good thing summer comes back every year." Boom winked. "And good thing neither of us is going anywhere."

Marina watched as Boom continued filming the others. "I'm sorry you weren't able to make the documentary for your dad."

Boom shrugged. "That's okay. Maybe we can make a new documentary at school. There's always gonna be some drama there. Would you . . . maybe want to do that with me?"

Thinking about school starting gave Marina that familiar stomachache, and that chest-tightening feeling she had been getting used to. The new school year was always a little scary. She'd have new teachers, and she might have tough homework. She'd have to adjust to seeing her school friends all over again. And, on top of that, she would start seeing a counselor, like Sam did—both with her moms and on her own. There were a lot of changes that would happen quickly in the next few weeks, and Marina wasn't sure if she was ready.

But at least Boom would be there, too. "Yes, Boom," Marina said. "I definitely want to keep making movies with you."

Boom let out a frustrated groan. "I'm going to miss this. We moved in too late. I can't believe summer is over."

Mama came up to stand behind them. "I'll miss it, too," she said, gently grasping Marina's shoulder.

There was a moment when Marina tensed up, almost shoved Mama's hand away. There was a moment when she really wanted to. She caught that moment, though, and thought about it. She thought about the conversations she and Mama—and Mom—were starting to have. She thought about the counselor they would speak to soon.

She didn't pull away. She leaned into Mama instead. Mama hugged her a little tighter.

"Sonny! Peter! We need to get ready to go!" their mom called over from the Badgers' back porch.

"Five more minutes!" called Pork from the lagoon.

"Ten more minutes!" called Cordelia right after.

"Fine! Ten more minutes, but then you're out of the water!"

The three kids in the water started cheering. Harbor and Sonny took the cue, too, racing each other to jump from the dock. When Sonny popped back out of the water, he pushed his hair out of his eyes and looked up at Sam. "Are you coming in?" he asked. "Come on. Come in with us!"

Sam put her pole down. She looked out at the water and back at Marina. She took a deep breath, counted to three, and jumped in.

Boom tugged at Marina's arm. "Come on. Us too!"

Marina let her best friend pull her across the deck.

They counted to three . . .

And joined the rest of her family in the water.

ACKNOWLEDGMENTS

I was out for a walk along the marshes by the lagoon where my parents live when I got a phone call from my agent, Jim McCarthy. He had just had a meeting with my team at Algonquin: my editor, Krestyna Lypen, and former publisher, Elise Howard. He said, "What are your thoughts on maybe writing something that could be a series?"

The three of them believed I'd be very good at it, and that I should give it a try. I thought about it the rest of that summer day, sitting out back with my view of the lagoon in Forked River. I thought about all the big family middle-grade series I loved. I thought about the type of family I might have some day. About the types of families represented in books that are currently being targeted and challenged and banned.

I want to thank Jim, Krestyna, and Elise, first and foremost, for planting the seed in my head that made me create the Ali-O'Connor family. I also want to thank them and everyone at Algonquin Young Readers for continuously proving to me that I can trust them to usher these books into the world with such determination and care, despite all the aforementioned book challenges and bans.

I also want to thank Andrew Sass, for always being the best partner in crime and writer buddy anyone could ask for. Our phones are going to burn out one of these days from all our texts during the most stressful of writing days, but it means the world to always have someone in my corner who understands.

To Alder Van Otterloo, Elm Dickson, Ez Symes-Smith, Elle Grenier, and Molly Kasperek: Our Twitter group chat was a lifesaver while drafting these Sunrise Lagoon books. I'm so lucky to have both this group of friends and a safe place to dump all my anxieties without judgment.

As always, a shout-out to my wife, Liz: You are forever my Theo and my wuffenloaf.

Mom and Dad: Obviously this book wouldn't exist without the house on the lagoon, our trips on the boat to Tices Shoal, and for all the Melleby quirks and traditions I stole to give to the Ali-O'Connors. And Matthew, too, since he was the first person to find the mussels while kayaking by the marshes.

And one last shout-out to every single middle schooler who has reached out to tell me your story: I still hear and see you, and I always will.

LOOK FOR SAM'S BOOK
IN THE
HOUSE ON SUNRISE LAGOON
SERIES!

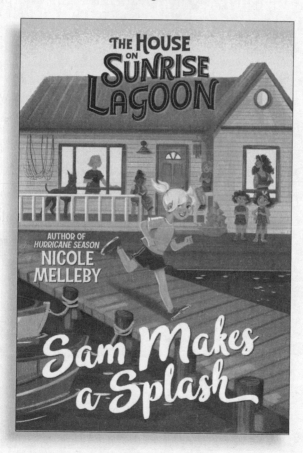

MORE UNFORGETTABLE STORIES FROM
NICOLE MELLEBY
ABOUT COURAGE, HOPE, LOVE
AND WHAT MAKES A FAMILY